Spirit on the Run

by

D.J. Vanas

TELEMACHUS PRESS

SPIRIT ON THE RUN

Cover designed by Telemachus Press, LLC

Cover art:
Copyright © 000002192619/iStockphoto/GBlakeley
Copyright © 000003506509/iStockphoto/Filmstroem
Copyright © 000018153579/iStockphoto/Mysticenergy

Published by Telemachus Press, LLC
http://www.telemachuspress.com

Visit the author website:
http://www.djvanas.com

ISBN: 978-1-939927-96-5 (eBook)
ISBN: 978-1-939927-97-2 (Paperback)

Version 2013.10.20

Printed in the United States of America

10 9 8 7 6 5 4 3 2 1

Praise for D.J. Vanas and Spirit on the Run

D.J. Vanas has poured his soul into this story. Each, word, sentence, paragraph and page of *Spirit on the Run* is a piece of his own spirit. He takes us into the dark pit that is grief and brings us out the other side and into the light of wisdom. It is a book that teaches us that there is a way out of the abyss. Vanas does here what all good stories do—he comforts us by telling us we are not alone.

Brian McDonald, Author of *Invisible Ink* and writer/director of *White Face*

Spirit on the Run is the compelling, hopeful story of a man coming to terms with a devastating loss. With an intense, emotionally honesty voice, D.J. Vanas deftly weaves together suspense, family drama, and spiritual adventure for a truly captivating read.

Kirk Farber, Author of *Postcards from a Dead Girl*

Spirit on the Run is an exciting inspirational novel of a Native American family man who seems to have it all, yet is haunted by his fractured, tragic past. His challenging journey for peace sparks hope for those who have suffered loss and gives courage to face the pain and heal. This sensational spiritual adventure reminds us that our hurts don't have to break us but instead can give us the courage to change, to lead a better even more fulfilling life. Anyone who has ever questioned or lost faith in the goodness of life or themselves will find renewal, restoration and the rebirth of hope!
LeAnn Thieman CSP, CPAE
Author of *Chicken Soup for the Soul: A Book of Miracles*

Insightful and hopeful, once again, D.J. uses his Native American culture to take us on a journey inside ourselves through the lens of Derek, his main character and gives us permission to look at how life can be encumbered and revived, as the engaging pages we read bring us into this mosaic family—challenged by their realities, yet buoyed by the possibilities that also surrounded them. I left the story with a greater appreciation of the capacity of the human family—a capacity for unselfishness which can be experienced wherever people gather.
Clifton L. Taulbert, Pulitzer-Nominated Author of *Once Upon A Time When We Were Colored* and *Eight Habits of the Heart*

Acknowledgements

I'd like to thank the Creator for blessing my journey with the joy and pain that has made it the adventure it is. Writing this novel has been one of the hardest things I've ever done. There were so many times I wanted to quit, but the memory of the baby son we lost has been a constant whisper to *keep going*. This story became a way to honor his life and I hope that it has.

I sincerely appreciate the time and insights of my original beta readers of the manuscript including: Lisa O'Quinn, Gyasi Ross, Dawn and Stephan Wolfert, Aaron Lawson, my mother-in-law Iris Rosario-Atkins and especially LeAnn Thiemann who has been the midwife in the birth of this novel. Her willingness to provide extensive feedback, support and encouragement to a fellow writer speaks volumes about her character and selflessness.

Thank you to John Tayer of Roche and Mary Lynn Eaglestaff of the Indian Health Service for sharing insights into the world of medical equipment sales.

Thank you to Rick Williams, former President and CEO of the American Indian College Fund, for his insight and instruction on the Lakota language—but even more so for his friendship, guidance and wisdom. He is truly my *Kola* and I'm proud to be his.

I'm grateful to my editors Pam Mellskog and Dawn Josephson for carving, hammering and polishing not only the manuscript into a better state, but the writer as well.

I'd also like to thank my incredible publishing team at Telemachus Press for not only their professionalism and attention to detail, but for their integrity, patience and guidance in bringing this story to life. Thank you Steve Jackson, Mary Ann Nocco, Terri and Steve Himes. You all are awesome.

To our great friends Troy, Dana and Allie Harting ... we don't know where we'd be without you, but it sure wouldn't be as much fun. Thanks for the years of supportive friendship, laughter and the spontaneous dance parties, from Paris to Colorado—they were medicine. And to Kevin Graefe, Ricardo Torres, George Woodruff, Dr. Karen Goodnight, and so many more friends who have all said things to me, whether they knew it or not, that meant so much in providing me strength during this process.

Thank you to my Mastermind group composed of Elaine Dumler, Fred Berns, Brad Montgomery, Jay Arthur, LeAnn Theiman and Sarah Michel. You all provided, throughout this project, either a hand to hold or swift kick in the rear and I sincerely appreciate both.

To my readers and followers, I have deeply appreciated your patience and persistence, asking often "when is your next book coming out?" and I'm proud to say, "Here it is!" I promise not to make you wait so long next time.

I'm forever grateful for my parents, Darrell and Mary Jo Vanas, for their example of hard work and sacrifice, for inspiring me to believe in myself no matter the odds and for their lifelong support and encouragement. I'm also grateful to my sister Kimberly and my brother-in-law Wesley Buchanan for their love and support and for the technical assistance during the times when my technology became my nemesis. I'd have thrown my computer out the window, several times, if it wasn't for you two.

To my daughters, Gabrielle and Isabella, I'll love you forever and more than I could ever say. No man in the world has been prouder to be a Daddy with gifts like you in my life. You keep me laughing, growing, thinking and expanding my capacity to love. You both are die-hard believers in who I am and what I do, enduringly patient with all my travels and I'll continue to work hard to honor that.

And to my rock, the love of my life, my beautiful wife Arienne. Your constant love, unwavering support, insights, laughter and companionship are gifts. You're the eye in my hurricanes and if it's a blessing to be married to someone who believes in us more than we do … then I'm blessed beyond words! It is an honor and joy to share the journey with you.

Dedication

To my three children, Gabrielle and Isabella—our treasures on earth—and Kieran, our treasure in heaven ... you're with me on every run.

To my beautiful wife, for my beautiful life ...

Table of Contents

Spirit on the Run

CHAPTER 1

"GET THAT SUMBITCH!" one of the boys screamed over the howl of the storm. Seven boys tore through the hedgerow that served as the border at the rear of the school campus, working as a pack in pursuit of their quarry. The pitiful creature they chased had barely escaped their fierce clutches. The seven pursuers had become a singular beast with a singular mind. This was a hunt that the pack relished.

The rain came down in sheets with a deafening roar but was drowned out each time the thunder exploded around them. The pack leader, a redhead with freckles, had a hint of an upturned grin. The wicked smirk exposed a row of yellowed teeth like a line of corn peeking from its husk. The vicious pack wore sneakers with tube socks, colored jeans and hooded zip-up sweatshirts—wolves in kids' clothing.

Lightning split the sky and popped like flashbulbs on the brown-skinned boy, momentarily freezing the image of the peeling iron-on decal of his Star Wars t-shirt and the frayed edges of hand-me-down jeans. This wasn't a race for glory or prizes, but for survival itself.

Derek Sorensen's frightened feet exploded the water in the puddles they hit. His legs worked like pistons in overdrive and his heart pumped madly, threatening to break the ties that held it in place. Every few steps, the boy's head whipped around with wide eyes.

Derek had nearly blacked out from the beating, the pounding fists and feet lost their color as they rained down on him and the angry shouting of the boys had lost sound. But on the edge of consciousness, he felt pulled to his feet by someone or something. The next moment, Derek was running, blindly at first, not only from panic but because his left eye was nearly swollen shut. His fattened lips had been split open, like overcooked sausages, in the middle of his wrecked face.

This late fall storm brought a cutting chill and a bruised sky. The boys behind Derek trampled soggy sassafras and oak leaves, puffing clouds of vapor in unison. They resembled a speeding locomotive with six cars behind the redheaded engine, racing on rails through the forest. Ahead, thorny vines clawed at his pants and flesh like hungry things. Sharp bolts of pain shot through his back and chest with each heaving breath. Ribs tended to do that when they were broken.

The pack steadily closed on their quarry. The adrenaline only seemed to be serving the pursuers now. It was only a matter of time.

Suddenly, a buzz filled the air, the telltale sign of a lightning strike. Maybe God was merciful after all. Derek assumed it would be a peaceful death, sudden and complete, like the calf he'd seen on a roadside last year, charred in places and bloated all over. Its legs stuck out like poles. His foster dad had mumbled, "Never knew what hit 'em Derek; no need to cry for it," as they drove by slowly on inspection.

The humming continued, as if the air itself was electrified. Derek felt as he did when he crawled around the carpet in his cotton pajamas. A static shroud surrounded him. He ran faster now, much faster, than he'd ever run before, as if he was flying over the terrain.

The boys in pursuit also got chicken skin from the electrified air, but ignored it. Rather than hitting the ground to lie flat—they'd been told by their kin, *buzzin' brings lightnin*—the boys continued tearing after their prey.

The boy closest in pursuit began running slower with his head jutted forward, squinting. He suddenly stopped and his mouth hung slack with wonder. What he saw didn't register. It couldn't. They had been running flat out when they burst through the underbrush into Mr. Thompson's fields. Recently harvested, the plots left behind nubs of vegetation and water-filled furrows that spilled over into shallow pools. But up ahead, Derek's feet no longer splashed through the puddles. It seemed his feet made no disturbance at all.

When the other boys caught up to their comrade, they leaned on their knees, panting hard. "What the hell, Simon!" Rory McCloud screamed through yellowed teeth and then gulped to catch his breath. He grabbed Simon by his shirt. "Damn it! You almost had him!" Simon didn't even turn his head to face his accuser. He could only stare blankly across the field at the woods that had just swallowed up their prey.

Derek eventually slowed to a stumbling jog that grew more uncoordinated. He had no idea how far he'd run or where he was. A twelve-year-old boy's sense of distance lingers in more familiar measures, like the walk to school or the drive to church. He recognized Mr. Thompson's field, an open space he had passed with his foster family on occasional trips to the city, but that was well over an hour ago.

Sharp pine, wet earth and rotting wood made the quiet forest fragrant but Derek couldn't smell any of it. His bloodied nose now filled with snot. He started to shiver from the frigid air, the exhaustion and from being a boy lost in the woods after nearly being killed by a schoolyard mob.

Nightfall approached and he wanted to get out of the rain that would soon become sleet. He regretted leaving his jacket on the hook in the classroom when he went out to the field after school. His adrenaline gone, Derek bore the full measure of his injuries. Some wounds felt sharp like stabbing nails while others throbbed like hammers on bone.

Derek staggered over piles of soppy leaves and pushed through bushes until he came to an inviting stand of trees. The changing color of a stand of red maples made a cheery umbrella in the middle of the woods. He plopped down between two tree trunks that grew strangely close. He hugged his drawn up knees and tried to conserve what little body heat he had left. Derek realized nature had no regard for the injured, sick or lost. It offered no solace, no breaks, not even for twelve-year-old boys.

The rain continued to fall; the dark continued to grow. Derek recalled a book he'd read in school about polar explorers that froze to death on their adventures. That seemed much nobler than dying of exposure after running from bullies.

His teeth chattered and his body stiffened in spasms. He was sure he wouldn't make it through the night but he wasn't upset. He'd heard freezing to death was like falling to sleep. He remembered seeing pictures in books of bodies half embedded in ice and frozen stiff, like mannequins at Woolworth's.

Whether he would die from a lightning strike or exposure, the result would be the same and not all bad. Maybe he would meet his real family in heaven. He suspected his wish was being granted as the air hummed around him again. The static returned to his skin and face. A warm bloom started in his chest and he began to feel as happy as the day he was adopted. *This was it.*

Despite the biting cold and rain, Derek felt like he was covered in the thick quilts of down his new parents kept in the trunk at the foot of their bed. He looked at his arms and saw steam rising. His skin was drying. He thought this may be the slowest lightning bolt in the history of the world.

Derek suddenly no longer felt alone, but protected and in the company of friends. He smiled with anticipation. He was going to heaven now and everything would be fine. No more pain. No more fear. No more sadness. Everything was going to be all right after all. This was it. He was sure of it now. He closed his eyes to see the most wonderful dreams a twelve-year-old boy could dream.

CHAPTER 2

"LIFE'S A BEAUTIFUL gift," the TV preacher said with a radiant smile. Derek, years later, sat on a bed in his darkened hotel room watching the flickering screen. After hearing that line, he reached for the glass holding a copper pool of liquid in the bottom. He took another sip, grimacing at the burn.

"What a joke. Try my life, preacher man," Derek slurred sarcastically as he sat the glass next to a greasy wrapper that recently covered a bacon cheeseburger. The fifth of whiskey was nearly drained, but Derek felt no closer to peace. As every other time, there had been no solace in this bottle. The drink filled no holes, replaced no losses.

Derek frequently found himself in this same scenario over the last year. Far from home in a strange hotel room, numbing the pain of his existence through booze, bad food and work. The constant grind of travel had left him hollowed out and alone with his thoughts and self-loathing. Cracked and sinking vessels keep going for a time before sliding beneath the waves. In his mind, he sailed the same course—overweight, unhappy and being pulled under by an emptiness he couldn't seem to escape.

Derek stumbled to his feet after switching off the TV and lumbered his way to the window. After pulling back the curtain, he shielded his eyes from a blinking neon sign. The pulsating purple light illuminated a large fly lying peacefully dead on its back in the window sill. The thing's buggy legs reached up toward him like a tiny grasping hand. He looked down with a furrowed brow and pushed the insect with his finger to make sure it wasn't pretending to be asleep. He didn't want another fake in the room sharing his hideout.

His gaze shifted beyond the light onto the dark empty street. Restlessly stepping back from the curtain, Derek's head lolled and his eyes searched for something that didn't exist in this room and never would. Derek plopped his fat body onto the mattress, which squeaked a scream of protest.

A whiskey burp erupted, a hot jet of gas from this human geyser, and burned the back of his throat. He opened his wallet and lovingly touched the family picture behind the plastic window. Nina stood radiantly next to Derek in the photo and their two girls, Bailey and Hannah, had the uncertain smile children offer up to strange photographers. Derek looked at his own grinning image with disgust. *That man is a lie* he thought. Derek snapped the wallet and his moistened eyes shut.

Derek turned on the TV and growled as he flipped through the channels. "What the hell is wrong with me?" He seemed to have every symptom described in every drug commercial promising a fix. Maybe if he watched long enough, he'd find the right pill to cure his ailments. In the meantime, he had his bottle.

Life was supposed to be better than laying here in a hotel bed watching *Sanford and Son* at 2:30 in the morning. He wondered what it would be like to go to sleep and never wake up, like the fly in the window sill.

Derek had a nice family, nice cars and a nice home in a nice neighborhood. It didn't make a dent in the dark mood he'd carried since the death of his son. It seemed like he was living someone else's good life, someone who actually deserved it. His anger was like a chipped tooth—ever present and immune to the tongue that ended up raw and bleeding when it desperately tried to rub it away. As he pulled up the sheets in his tightened fists, he grew bitter all over again about the usual things: his job, his past, the world around him and the loss of his son—but mostly bitter about himself.

Derek's mind ran in circles to the soundtrack of a TV infomercial until his near-empty glass slipped from his hand and tumbled onto the hotel room carpet, leaving a dark stain. His thoughts followed in the same way and then faded into nothingness …

Derek let out a long sigh as he rubbed his stubbly face in the mirror. He heard the kids and Nina downstairs and smelled the aroma of coffee, but still carried the rank remnants of stale whiskey in the back of his throat from the morning before. Yesterday had been a hangover blur on the journey home. But even today, his head throbbed like an eggshell ready to burst. Though only in his late thirties, he felt older. He looked older.

The cheery weather man on TV in the bedroom announced, "Good morning, San Diego. Another beautiful day today. The forecast is 78 and sunny."

Derek mockingly repeated the announcement under his breath. He leaned forward and ran his fingers through his ebony hair, seeing a few white ones. He looked at himself from different angles, but they all looked fat. He lumbered off to go find some clothes that still fit.

Derek went to his dresser and stared at the familiar figure on top—a small carving of an angel with wire wings, tenderly holding a baby boy in her arms. The faceless figure was dressed in a flowing gown and clutched the infant as if they'd melted together, connected forever. It always put a lump in Derek's throat but he couldn't bring himself to remove the figurine. Like an amputee longing to scratch an itch on his phantom leg for relief, Derek wanted to touch his son. He gingerly reached for the statue as Nina's voice jolted him from the moment.

"Honey! Come on, or you're going to be late. Skip will be here in a minute." Nina went back to making lunches for Bailey and Hannah to take to school.

Derek walked down the stairs and mustered a smile for the girls. He grabbed his cup of coffee and carelessly kissed Nina on the cheek.

"Thanks. I'll be home late again tonight," he said, his voice thick and gravelly.

Derek's buddy, Skip Tanner, rapped on the back door and entered with the flair of a prince. After a deep bow to the girls, he winked at Nina.

"Is my liege ready?" he asked in his best English accent. Derek rolled his eyes as the girls giggled.

"After school, we've got a parent teacher conference with Bailey's teacher," Nina said.

"I said I'll be home late," Derek replied and reached for his briefcase.

Nina looked crestfallen. "Well, yeah, I know. I just …"

"I told you, I can't." Derek said.

Skip made funny faces at the girls to smooth the awkward moment. Derek threw a quick obligatory wave goodbye as he took a sip of his coffee and pushed Skip through the door.

"What's a liege, Mommy?" Hannah asked.

The two men walked out to Skip's car, a battered pile of parts that had enjoyed its best years when Reagan was president. The paint chips that stubbornly remained on its body were light gray, but at one time had been black … or maybe blue. Derek doubted even Skip knew the original color.

"When the hell are you going to get a new car?" Derek asked.

"Every time it's my turn to drive, you ask the same question and I give the same answer. She's my baby," and he lovingly leaned on the roof of his '87 Honda Accord with outspread arms.

"When are you going to settle down and get married?" Derek asked as he absently stared out the window at the palm trees and traffic.

Skip rolled his eyes. "You're like a broken record, Derek. I told you, when Nina divorces you and is available, let me know."

That used to be the running joke. But now, it wasn't so funny. Ever since the death of their infant son last year, the couple had been on the roughest patch since they wed ten years ago. Skip sensed the tension and quickly recovered.

"Come on Derek, I'm married to my work, you know that."

"Yeah, and this ugly car," Derek replied, half smiling.

In many ways, Skip was married to work. It was his occupation, hobby and passion. He saved and invested all the money he earned, lived in a tiny townhouse and drove a relic. He always talked about his life *some* day. *Some* day he'd find the right woman. *Some* day he'd buy a big house on the beach and sail around the world. In the meantime, he just kept working, saving and waiting for *some* day.

"Knock it off, Skip," Derek said impatiently. "Not while we're driving."

Skip's thumb flew over the keys of his cell phone. He alternated his view from the road to the device and back again in a manic motion, like nodding yes over and over again with his eyes only.

"Almost … done," Skip said slowly to buy time.

"You need to shut that stupid thing off once in awhile," Derek said.

"What, like you?"

"Yeah, like me," Derek said.

"Well, I wanted to give you a heads up about the Mercy Regional account. They griped to Sedgewick about the delays and not being able to reach you. Now he's going to be griping to you about it," Skip said.

Derek's face turned dour.

"I told them I'd get around to it. I just had a lot of …" he said, trailing off to a mumble.

"You shoulda had *your* phone on more," Skip said. He back-pedaled as soon as the words spilled out. "Hey, I'm not busting your balls. I'm just telling you what I know."

When the two got to Global Medix, Mr. Sedgewick intercepted them right off the elevator. Skip glanced supportively at Derek before departing to his office.

"What the hell is going on with this Mercy Regional account, Derek?" Sedgewick demanded. "They've got a pile of orders higher than a phonebook and can't get a hold of you." His fiery red hairpiece always seemed to highlight his anger in these moments.

"I told them I'd take care of it," Derek said.

Sedgewick breathed heavily, gearing up for a rousing speech.

Charles Sedgewick supervised Derek and Skip. He dressed sharply but sported a ridiculous toupee that resembled a golfer's cap more than hair. The toupee helped him, a man in his late-50s, to relive the glory days of his hair's youth. So despite the white strands streaking his once-red sideburns, he insisted on being forever red—nature be damned.

Otherwise, Sedgewick practiced a no-nonsense approach to life, reflecting his Midwestern upbringing. He had been an All-American tight end in college and wanted to coach. But his overbearing dad had other plans for Charles that involved getting him an internship and eventually a job at Global Medix.

Sedgewick made the most of it and lived out his coaching fantasy as a driven sales manager. He ran his staff as if they were a football team. Though usually a nice enough guy, he didn't mince words and often skirted the boundaries of office decorum and political correctness.

The management tolerated him for two reasons. One, he was a company super star who brought wealth to shareholders, and two, he was nearing early retirement.

Derek stood somberly, looking down. "It was on my agenda for this week. I was going to take care of it."

"Jesus H. Christ, Derek! You should have handled this three weeks ago," Sedgewick barked. Sensing his voice rising and remembering what he learned in his mandatory anger management class, he took a deep breath and spoke in a lower tone. "Seriously, Derek. This is way overdue, and this hasn't been the only account," he said.

Sedgewick gulped and attempted to be delicate.

"Listen, we all still feel bad about your son, Derek. But that was almost a year ago and life goes on. We're trying to run a business here. Are you still part of this team or not?"

"Yes sir," Derek answered.

"Good. Then let's see some hustle out there," Sedgewick said, shoving his hand full of invoices and orders to within inches of Derek's beach ball-sized belly. "Handle this. *Today.*"

Sedgewick reached up to smooth his hairpiece and confirm its proper position. He usually ended conversations this way.

Derek took the paperwork and walked to his office, plopping down in his chair with an annoyed grunt. He looked down at the cell phone on his desk as it blinked, buzzed and vibrated across the smooth surface to indicate he had voicemail. The flashing amber light drew in Derek's gaze until the walls begin to collapse in on him. He closed his eyes and his hands began to tremble. Everything suddenly faded away ...

Derek pushed through the double doors to the NICU, the neonatal intensive care unit. He'd rushed to this hospital as soon as he landed at Lindbergh Field.

The crisis hit during his flight from California to Colorado on a sales call. When the plane landed in Denver, Derek turned on his cell phone and listened with increasing worry to panicked voicemail messages from Nina and her mother.

Nina was six months pregnant with their third child, their first son. Nina had gone into sudden preterm labor and needed to be rushed to the hospital by ambulance.

The calls to Derek were a rush of confusing words washed with terror, trying to explain the unimaginable. All he knew was that his son had been born by emergency C-section and weighed two pounds, seven ounces. His son had to be resuscitated after delivery, but was now stable.

Derek caught the next flight home and rushed to the hospital. Because Nina still slept in her recovery room, he visited the NICU first. He took a deep, shaky breath and shook hands with Dr. Tobias White.

"Hello, Mr. Sorensen. I'm Dr. White and I just want you to know, we're doing all we can for your son."

Derek could tell the doctor was trying to be optimistic but seemed hesitant, even guarded.

"He's right over here," Dr. White said as he guided Derek to a small Plexiglass crib surrounded by high-tech machinery, blinking lights and a chirping monitor that might seem alien to others, but was all too familiar to Derek. After all, he sold this equipment to the hospital, but he never imagined it would serve his own child.

Engulfed in a tangle of tubes, wires and medical tape was the tiniest person Derek had ever seen. His son's chest fluttered in rhythm with the ventilator. He wore a knitted blue cap over his dark corn silk hair. He had perfect, beautiful features with big feet like his daddy's. Patches of fine body hair, typical of premature babies, grew over his nearly translucent skin.

Alternating waves of joy of his son's birth and fear for his future washed over Derek. He threw his hand up to his mouth and in vain tried to hold back choking sobs ...

Derek rubbed his eyes to clear the flashback and reached for the phone. Nina had left him a message to remind him of the appointment they had tomorrow with the grief and marriage counselor.

Derek hated going. He found the experiences to be painfully invasive and useless. He wondered, sometimes out loud to Nina, why they were paying all this money and wasting all this time for nothing. That usually started an argument and, according to Nina, would justify the need for the counseling sessions all over again.

Nina and Derek had enjoyed a wonderful marriage until Cole's death last year. Now their relationship was strained and frozen in time. They couldn't move forward and they couldn't go back, stuck in a limbo of loss. It was as if they were holding their breath, waiting and desperately hoping for a change.

The next day, the counseling session quickly morphed into an elaborate game of hide-and-seek of Derek's emotions. Minutes into it, he rolled his wedding ring around and around with his thumb. Maybe it was because the counselor, Katherine, was a woman and Derek felt outnumbered. Maybe it was because she seemed too syrupy to be sincere. Whatever it was, Derek didn't care much for their counselor. He wouldn't say it out loud because he knew it would only start another squabble with Nina and justify the sessions. Instead, he followed what he had done as a foster kid—go with the flow and don't make waves.

"Derek, can you tell me more about your childhood? How was your relationship with your parents? Er, I mean your adopted parents." Katherine corrected herself, which annoyed Derek even more.

"My *parents* are great people. My childhood was fine." Derek had carried an inescapable frustration his whole life—his own skin. Derek was Native American and his physical features made that obvious, though he never knew to what tribe he belonged, let alone his biological family. Being born in Oklahoma, it could have been any one of the dozens of tribes represented in the state. It was as if he'd been issued a suit of brown skin at birth, but with no explanation or instructions, destined to be a generic Indian.

As a child, he often felt like he had been born nowhere to no one and by default was a no one headed nowhere himself. He drifted in and out of foster care for the first eight years of his life. He had been in twelve different homes during that time, many of them abusive. Derek didn't attach himself to much of anything or anyone. The less he invested in the situation, the easier it was to endure the beatings, the neglect and the next move.

Everything seemed temporary.

Still, when the Sorensen's took him in, Derek felt more at home than anywhere he'd ever been. Martha and Don lived in Bixby, a nearly all-white country town in rural southern Oklahoma. After their own two children had grown up and moved away, they'd decided to become foster parents.

Martha and Don both had very fair complexions. Despite the stark physical differences, they quickly bonded with Derek. They were drawn to his dark, intelligent eyes, and though stubborn, his sense of wonder and curiosity were infectious. Derek also brought welcome chaos into their quiet home.

They knew he was tough, but they also knew he needed love. What they lacked in money and means, they tried to make up for in compassion. Like coaxing a scared kitten out of the corner, Martha and Don patiently and lovingly showed Derek he could trust them.

Soon after Derek had come to live with them, Martha noticed several long, raised scars of newly grown flesh as she helped him get ready for bed after a bath. The bright pink welts looked like earthworms stretched across the surface of his brown skin where the extension cord had bit deeply.

Martha's horror only grew when she noticed various other marks and scars in different stages of healing. Small, chunky circles told of old cigarette burns. Large, faded bruises suspiciously shaped like the front face of a fist were on his upper thighs and chest. She couldn't imagine the terror this little boy had experienced and she never would. He refused to talk about it to anyone. Loud noises and voices made Derek visibly nervous and caused him to stare blankly into the distance. Seeing these signs of trauma connected her and Don in a visceral way to the child and they vowed to protect and love him for as long as he'd let them.

In time, the scars and bruises healed, but the damage done to Derek remained within and was deeper and more severe than any of them realized. Abuse had made him outwardly tough but internally fragile. He became apprehensive, distrustful of others and himself, doubtful, angry and mostly scared. Always scared.

During one visit to the grocery store, Derek had run ahead, eager to help his new parents collect their needed items. When Don rounded the aisle corner, he found Derek quietly halted in front of a pungent display for Cogburn's Cologne and Aftershave. The blood had drained from the little boy's face. He trembled and dripped sweat, staring in horror at the bottles. When Don asked if he was okay, he noticed a dark patch blooming as Derek wet his green Toughskin pants.

Don reached down for Derek's hand and gently led him away from the display. The child was like a zombie in tow. Don could only suspect one of the bastards that had laid hands on Derek wore the scent.

Later in life Derek claimed he didn't remember most of these things. Don and Martha figured he'd blocked them out due to trauma. They believed God had been merciful in this regard.

The temporary foster care soon evolved into Derek's adoption and permanent placement. Derek started to finally build good memories, but he always worried and wondered how long it would last, never trusting it could. It was a fear that remained.

One night, shortly after Derek's adoption was finalized, Don came home with a bruised and bloody hand. He gently sent Derek to his room before telling Martha what happened. The boy promptly planted his ear at the gap between floor and door to learn that a so-called friend questioned why Don and Martha would adopt a "prairie nigger" instead of a white baby. Though he'd never hit another person in his life, Don had cracked a tooth out of the man's mouth for that remark.

Martha, always kind and calm, immediately picked up the phone and lashed the person on the other end of it with an acrid, cutting diatribe that made clear what was what—and calling the heavens down in the process. When Derek heard them defending him, he felt an unfamiliar tingle in his chest. For the first time in his life, Derek loved someone. In time, he called them Mamma and Pappa Don.

When he got older he embarked on the pilgrimage many adopted kids make. He tried to find his birth parents. Along the way he suffered through mysterious explanations, countless phone calls and conflicting paperwork that led nowhere. He chased smoke and shadows. After years of red tape and frustration, he decided he was blessed with the family he had and let it rest. But the fact that his biological parents gave him up remained ever present, a splinter in his mind that couldn't be removed.

Now sitting with his wife on a counselor's couch, Derek patiently reiterated, with thinly veiled condescension, that his upbringing with the Sorensens was just fine.

"Do they still live in Oklahoma?" Katherine pressed.

"In the same house too," Derek answered, pushing his tongue hard against the roof of his mouth to restrain his building wrath.

The rest of the session went as expected. Katherine tried to heal the wounded. Nina tried to be supportive of Derek. Derek tried to leave as soon as possible to go anywhere, even back to work, and to keep his mouth shut to avoid prolonging the agonizing session.

On the way home from the appointment, Derek and Nina drove in silence for the first few minutes. Derek would have been happy to continue that way all the way home, but Nina writhed inside.

Nina tried her best to stay positive and supportive even as Derek grew despondent and detached. After the loss, everyone seemed to be healing and moving on, except for Derek. It was like watching a houseplant die despite heroic efforts to save it. She worried about their marriage as the gulf between them grew wider.

"Why do you always do that to her? She's only trying to help," Nina finally said.

"Yeah, and we pay her a lot of money for that help," Derek quipped. Silence filled the minivan for the next few minutes.

"I've got Mom watching the kids next Friday when we go to Tom and Lisa's," she said, holding her breath.

"Come on, Nina. All Tom ever talks about is real estate. I could give a rat's ass about his latest buy or sell, and Lisa's so busy running her mouth she wouldn't notice if the house burned down around her." Derek rolled his hands on the steering wheel. "I feel like telling them both just to shut the ..."

"They're our friends, Derek," Nina said indignantly. "We should spend time with the ones we have left."

"What the hell is that supposed to mean?" Derek aggressively weaved the minivan through traffic.

"It means we never do anything anymore. We never get together with anyone!"

Derek responded with silence. Nina moved her hand over to his.

"We're all still hurting too," she said.

Derek moved his hand away. "I know," he conceded.

"I could help if you'd let me, if you talked to me," Nina pleaded.

Derek used the moment to be cruel. "Well that's what we have Katherine for, isn't it? So we can *talk* about our issues."

Nina recoiled in anger. "That's not fair, Derek."

"What's not fair is not asking me before you signed us up for this shrink course, Nina," Derek fired back.

"Ask you! Ask you? You weren't even talking to me or the girls the first month after it happened!"

"Just stop. I don't want to talk about it," he said.

Exasperated, Nina looked out her window at the ocean. Her tears reflected in the glass and looked as if they were falling into the sea, adding to what she'd cried over the last year. Derek got his wish. They drove in silence the rest of the way home.

"Hi Mom," Nina said as she walked in the front door with Derek following quietly behind her.

Kay dared not ask how it went after seeing by Nina's puffy, red eyes. "The girls are fed and Bailey's just finishing her homework."

Kay hugged Nina and then turned to Derek.

"Hey, ya big lug. Give your mother-in-law a peck," she said to lighten the mood.

Derek bent down, hugged her and kissed her cheek.

"Hi Kay," he mumbled. Derek would have known it was Kay even if he were blind. She always smelled faintly of lilacs from the same perfume she'd worn since Derek and Nina were dating. "Thanks for watching the girls."

"Anytime, you know that," Kay replied as she gathered her things.

The chunky stones in her earrings swung wildly around her silvery bob as she playfully asked no one in particular, "Now who's taken my purse?"

Bailey smiled as she did her homework at the kitchen table. Hannah giggled and squinted at *Dora the Explorer* on TV to keep her secret. Kay soon chased little Hannah and tickled her when she caught her.

"Goodnight, all. Love you," Kay said over her shoulder as Nina walked her to the door.

"Love you Grandma," the girls said in unison as Derek searched the fridge for a beer. Nina opened the door and waited for Kay to fish car keys from her purse.

"Goodnight Mom," Nina said.

"Goodnight Nina. I'll see you next Friday," Kay answered and turned to leave.

"No. Don't worry about it. We're not going," Nina said as she leaned, defeated, in the doorway.

Kay turned around. "It's okay, *Sakura*," she said and grabbed Nina's hand. "It takes longer for some than others."

The two tightly embraced. Kay climbed into her Ford Taurus, pulled out of the driveway and blew a kiss.

Nina walked back into the kitchen to see Hannah holding Derek's hand and jumping up and down.

"Come on, Daddy, let's go exploring!" she squealed.

Derek looked less than excited and mumbled that he was too tired to play. At age five, the little girl was chock full of life and often spotted magic in the ordinary. She searched for treasure in the bathtub, saw animals in the clouds and claimed she gained superpowers when she ate her morning cereal.

The energetic kindergartener was also a daddy's girl through and through. That fact broke Nina's heart as she watched Hannah begging Derek for his time these days.

"Here, put this on Daddy," Hannah said, offering him a construction paper hat she made him. "It's your special hat!"

Derek took the hat but declined to wear it.

"Wear it, Daddy," she pleaded.

"I don't want to wear it," Derek snapped. "I'm tired and I don't want to play right now."

Hannah looked dejected. When she took the hat, tears welled in her eyes.

Nina bit her lip in frustration. Feeling like the Dutch boy at the dike, she let the moment pass without comment and moved to help Bailey with her homework.

Everyone joked that Bailey was an old soul already. At age nine, she tended to be quieter and more independent than other kids her age. Nina suspected that Bailey often brooded on the meaning of life.

"Derek, Bailey wants to show you the sculpture she made in school today," Nina said.

"No I don't," Bailey muttered and looked up, irritated.

"Come on, Bailey. It's beautiful. Show your dad," Nina continued, with her eyes willing Bailey to fetch the craft. "Your dad wants to see it, don't you, Derek?"

She looked at her husband, but he only shrugged vacantly as he watched Hannah pick up her toys. Bailey noticed her dad's reaction and lowered her head to finish her homework. She had made a wonderful clay sculpture of an ostrich, but Bailey seemed to not want to share her art with anyone uninterested.

Nina grew frustrated and ordered the girls upstairs to get ready for bed. She waited until they were in their rooms before turning to Derek.

"When you do it to me, that's one thing. But when you do it to the kids, Derek …"

Unable to finish, she went upstairs after the kids and left him standing in the kitchen, alone.

CHAPTER 3

THE NEXT MORNING, Derek lay in bed long after Nina and the kids got up to start their day. He watched the ceiling fan slowly turning and his mind wandered, as it often did, to thoughts of his departed son. He missed him every day. He often imagined what he would have looked like, how it would have been to wrestle with him or take him fishing.

He rubbed his ever-growing belly and yawned. He rolled over and looked at the clock that read 10:07 a.m. but Derek had no inclination to get out of bed. He knew Nina and the girls would let him rest, especially after last night, which made him feel deserted.

When he reflected on his son, Derek often revisited the workings of the universe and of God. Was God punishing him for something in his past? Why did Cole have to leave them? Even as an infant did he see something lacking in Derek? Why did life seem to magically work out for some and be so agonizing for others? Derek always pondered the same questions, hoping for answers that never came.

No matter how hard he tried there remained an ever-present aching hole in his heart that he couldn't fill or heal. He felt cheated. God had come like a thief in the night to rob him of his son. He clenched his scarred fists around the blankets, thinking of how many times in his life he'd used those tools to solve his problems. Derek wished it was that easy now, to be able to punch these feelings away, to knock them out of his life. He rolled over into a fetal position, aware of the self-pity washing over him.

In his mind he saw an image of a round-faced boy with sad, almond shaped eyes. The boy's brown skin and a black crew cut hair set him apart from the other schoolboys. He slowly walked to school in worn out clothes and carried his lunch in a tattered paper sack. As he walked close to a group of kids, one of them lunged out and slapped Derek on the head to an explosion of laughter from the others.

"Good morning, idiot!"

Even now, his blood ran hot at the recollection. Derek remembered the kid's freckled face, auburn hair and large, yellowed teeth bared just inches from his face. Mostly, he remembered Rory McCloud's sickening, menacing laugh.

The violence had become a morning tradition that Derek endured for weeks. But one morning, in an explosion of humiliation and rage, Derek belted Rory and watched with surprise as the kid stumbled backward with two rivers of red pouring from his nose.

Derek hoped retaliating would halt the bullying. Instead, it sparked a war with Rory, who recruited other boys into the fray. The attacks continued into high school and though he won a few fights, his resistance didn't change the course of the constant onslaught from every direction. Like trick birthday candles, just when he seemed to put out the fires with one group of kids, another conflagration emerged, and always led by Rory. Apparently the kids of town needed an emotional punching bag and Derek became the perfect candidate—poor, Indian and adopted.

Derek winced remembering how teachers and coaches hauled him in front of the Sorensens time after time for fighting. A few times, the police delivered Derek to their doorstep, gripping his shirt collar and holding him out front, like a cat that caught a mouse. Growing up as an Indian kid in a white family had its challenges and Derek got more than his share of harassment. Being poor made it worse. There were times he'd wanted to kill Rory McCloud. There were times he'd wanted to kill himself.

Had it not been for growing up in small town Oklahoma, Derek might have accumulated a juvenile delinquent rap sheet. But the town thought the world of the kindly Sorensens and felt empathy for Derek's past and present troubles. Most tended to shake their heads and look the other way, reluctant to add any burden to the struggling family.

The situation made Derek an outcast on either side of the color divide. The few other Indian kids at his school called him an apple, red on the outside and white on the inside, ignorant of his culture and even his tribe. In turn, they ignored him. He wasn't one of them. They avoided Derek as if he could infect them with the same disgraced reputation and castaway eyes.

One the other hand, many of the white kids gave Derek plenty of attention, but not the kind anyone wants. They called him a variety of repugnant names, the kindest being Injun Derek or Sorensen the Savage. Derek always had guilt over facing his family after fights, but there was a dark satisfaction in hurting those who would hurt him.

Derek found solace in schoolwork, immersing himself into books and learning. It was an arena where he excelled, something he could control. His performance caught the eyes of local and state colleges and allowed him an escape from his past. He started life over again in college, finding peace in being anonymous in a new location.

"Daaaaad, get up!" Bailey shouted from downstairs. "Skip is here!"

Derek quickly fumbled for his robe and stumbled into his slippers, cursing under his breath, "It's Saturday for Chrissakes."

Derek stomped down to the living room and saw Skip focused intently on the coffee table full of paperwork in front of him, pointing at a document with his left hand but texting madly with his right. Derek rolled his eyes. Skip wore slacks, a shirt and a Dallas Cowboys tie.

"Were you at work today?" Derek asked but already knew the answer.

"Sure was," Skip answered as he sipped from his latte. "I got all this together for you for your Houston meeting."

Derek both admired and envied Skip for his drive. Derek put in long hours too, but rather than work, he used the time as an escape from the rest of his life. Skip, on the other hand, was like a machine: productive and efficient.

Derek's fifteen-year friendship with Skip started at their orientation at Global Medix, where they were both new hires out of college. But the connection between the two went much deeper than co-workers. They shared a similar background of childhood challenges. Skip had grown up, in his words, poor white trash, in a trailer park in Texas to parents who loved him and his brother dearly but were always broke. Skip resented his parents for being poor though they had showered him with love. He'd hated shopping at the local thrift store and getting handouts from the community.

Skip's relentless drive to escape poverty and his parent's situation brought him a chance to go to college. His parents spent all they had to send Skip to school, but Skip had to drop out as a sophomore when the money ran dry. The job he held on the side couldn't sustain tuition. Skip returned home bitter and barely spoke to his forlorn parents though they promised to find a way to send him back to school.

Within weeks of his return home, Skip's parents died in a car accident. The tragedy left Skip and his younger brother alone, but with some money from a meager life insurance policy. Skip's parents were able to provide in death what they couldn't provide in life. The sad irony wasn't lost on Skip as he used the money to finish school and then send his younger brother as well.

Now Skip worked obsessively so he never lacked money again. "You can't live on love" is what he liked to say, not believing money and love could co-exist. His philosophy kept women at arm's length, and seeing it as fear of commitment, they eventually moved on. Skip wasn't afraid of commitment; he was just busy. Dreadfully busy. He worked feverishly to save for a wonderful tomorrow.

Skip's sense of humor and Texas twang made the longest days go by quickly, but his real value to Derek came in times like these. Skip knew Derek was in deep water with the Mercy Regional account and wasn't about to stand by and let his friend drown in it. So instead he came over on this Saturday to prep Derek on the latest equipment and help him get sharp for the presentation. Like flashcards in grade school, Skip would show slide shots of equipment and Derek would rattle off descriptions, features, performance and price points.

"What about this one?" Skip said with the approach of a puppy trainer.

"I have no idea." Derek sipped his coffee. "Haven't seen it before."

"That's R2D2!" Hannah shouted to her doll.

"C'mon, honey, Daddy's working." Nina hustled Hannah out of the room like a bouncer, switching between reason and gentle force on the resistant child.

The two men went back and forth with the pictures and the information until they both seemed bored. Skip held up a picture of a machine that would have resembled a ham radio to a casual onlooker, but Derek knew it too well and his stomach lurched. He and this machine had a history.

"Helloooo. Earth to Derek. What is it?" Skip looked down and thumbed a text while he waved the picture at Derek. He hadn't seen the pinched look on Derek's face.

"It's a neonatal vent," Derek finally answered.

"What *kind* of neonatal ventilator?"

Derek was silent.

Skip looked up with raised eyebrows like an expectant professor.

"It's an XTM5000 Infant Defender," Derek cringed at the last word, false advertising at best.

"And?"

"And I'm tired. Look, I've got shit to do today and you've … got to get a life."

"Okay, man. Geez, you're as grumpy as a hairless goat in the heat." Skip finished his text, one-thumbed, and began shuffling the paperwork into a pile.

Normally Derek cracked up at Skip's ridiculous comebacks, but the image had reopened a dark pit in Derek's mind.

It was Tuesday morning and Derek's stomach was in a knot. He was at Mercy Regional Hospital in Houston preparing for a sales presentation on Global Medix equipment to a panel of doctors and hospital administrators. The incredible pressure of a large invisible hand gripped his heart since this was the client he'd disappointed. He'd delayed their paperwork and took weeks to return their phone calls. The truth was, Derek didn't want this client or this sale. He tried to get pulled off the account. The fact that Sedgewick had decided to sit in on this meeting put Derek into a full blown panic.

"Just take a deep breath and go over the stuff I dropped off this weekend," Skip said through the phone.

Derek stood in the hallway, clutching his cell phone like it was life itself. Rivulets of sweat fell down the back of his neck and the side of his head.

"Did you go over it?" Skip asked.

"I went over it, but it's the … what I mean is that I just …" Derek stumbled through his thoughts.

"We're ready, Derek," Sedgewick said, poking his head out of the door. "I got 'em warmed up in here, now go get 'em Chief." He disappeared back into the room. Derek resented the playful but condescending reference his boss often made to his Native heritage. Today was no different.

Derek quickly ended his call with Skip and shut off his phone. He swallowed hard and as he reached for the door handle, he noticed his hand shaking. He tried in vain to review the key sales points in his mind as he entered the room. He grabbed the remote that would control the computer slideshow and did his best to fake a smile as he introduced himself, inhaling a wave of coffee, perfume and the aroma of new carpet.

The meeting started well and Sedgewick even seemed pleased, occasionally winking at Derek to show his approval. Clearly he wanted Derek to succeed here. A failure at this presentation would not only mean disaster for the Mercy Regional account, but it would also mean Sedgewick would have to slap Derek with harsh consequences neither wanted.

"Up next we have an equipment roster specifically for your NICU," Derek said. His heart raced and his mouth turned to cotton. The smells of the room had become noxious. He cleared his throat and began to go through each piece of equipment, each type of sensor, monitor and diagnostic tool in succession. When he finally got to the ventilator, he stared blankly at the image on the screen. He could hear his own pulse in his ears as the piece of equipment seemed to spring to life. Derek imagined its lights blinking and the room melted away …

Cole's chest fluttered in sync with the high frequency ventilator to which he was connected, the XTM5000 Infant Defender. Derek and Nina hovered over the incubator, each placing a finger in each of Cole's tiny hands. They had been a constant presence around the clock for the past three days, hoping and praying for good news. They both were exhausted and had dark circles under their reddened eyes. The Sorensens had flown out from Oklahoma to watch the girls. Kay had played a catch all, delivering take out, do-nuts and support to Derek and Nina and checking on Don and Martha and the girls.

Derek and Nina talked to Cole, sang to him and prayed with him. Derek continued to sing *You Are My Sunshine* over and over again, finding comfort in the repetition and being too tired to sing anything else. They'd move aside for the NICU nurses doing their frequent checks and then quickly rush back to Cole's side, kissing his feet, hands and any part of his little body that wasn't covered in tape, tubes or wires.

Between tears and prayers, cat naps and countless cups of bad coffee, Derek and Nina held vigil. Cole was stable, but fighting an infection. Derek and Nina eagerly awaited results from a brain ul-trasound. Dr. White and Dr. Mackenzie approached somberly be-hind the couple. "We need to talk with you both. We've got a meeting room reserved behind the NICU." Derek and Nina looked at the doctors and then at each other, worried.

Derek bent down to Cole and kissed his forehead, "We'll be right back little man." Nina kissed Cole's cheek and took Derek's hand to follow the doctors. They were ushered into a meeting room connected to the NICU and sat down in stiff chairs under merciless lights.

"We were hopeful about the ultrasound done earlier today," Dr. White said. "But what we got back didn't look good."

The words were ice water thrown in Derek and Nina's faces. The doctors looked at each other, seeming uncomfortable.

"Your son is not only fighting an infection, but has also developed a bilateral brain bleed. A level 3 or 4, we're not sure."

Nina looked bewildered.

"What does that mean?" she asked. Derek sat silently, unable to swallow. He knew what it meant.

"It means your son has a severe bleed in each hemisphere of his brain. Some bleeding in preemies is typical, but in your son's situation, his vessels are collapsing and he's bleeding out."

The doctors grabbed for charts as they explained the medical situation, clearly more comfortable in that realm. They showed scans of Cole's brain and explained that the large clouds of white that dominated the image were blood. The doctor's voices droned on incoherently in Derek's mind.

"What's the prognosis?" Derek finally blurted, unable to tolerate any more of what seemed like a sales pitch to sell a shred of hope. Nina seemed to be in shock with her face wet, but emotionless. The doctors again nervously looked at each other.

"Well, we don't know, Mr. Sorensen," Dr. Mackenzie admitted. "We're doing all we can, but ..."

"Is he going to die?" Derek was startled by his own words but needed to know.

"He could," Dr. White answered, cornered with nowhere else to go with a response.

The rest of the conversation discussed options and possible outcomes if Cole survived at all. Derek couldn't hear or understand most of it, but did catch words like *painful corrective surgeries*, *blindness*, *severe retardation* and *cerebral palsy*. He was in a nauseous daze, like the time he'd fallen off the monkey bars and hit his head on the concrete in grade school. The persistent aroma of rubbing alcohol, inescapable even in the meeting room, was like a gaseous terror and hung with its awful odor in the back of his throat.

After the meeting ended, Derek and Nina walked back into the NICU in a shell-shocked trance. They assumed their positions at their son's side, held his hands and didn't say a word for hours.

"Derek!" Sedgewick growled and then meekly smiled at the concerned faces of the hospital staff and administrators.

Derek quickly tried to compose himself as he looked around. "Bottomline, ladies and gentlemen is that this machine … will … save lives." Derek's voice crumbled as the filthy lie left his mouth. Suddenly his throat constricted and he couldn't speak or breathe. It was the same cursed machine to which his son had been connected. Today would have been Cole's first birthday. He desperately looked for something, anything to save him from this moment. He dropped the remote and bolted for the door and didn't stop until he got to the men's room.

Derek violently wretched into the sink and then looked up at the image in the mirror. His fat brown face streaked with tears and sweat. He wanted to explode. *Why did so many other parents get to take their baby home? Did the doctors really do everything they could? God is a thief, a dirty thief.* These thoughts peppered Derek's mind like the stinging strikes he endured from childhood bullies. He was losing it. He could hear footsteps rapidly approaching as the door burst open.

"What the hell was that about?" Sedgewick cried. "Do you realize what you might have just done?"

Still lost in his own turmoil, Derek stared blankly at the swirling water, wanting to follow it down the drain.

"I have to go back in there and fix your screw up!" Sedgewick's fury was hitting the boiling point and his toupee slightly shifted on his head. All he'd learned in anger management was being tested. "We'll discuss the future of your employment with Global Medix when we get back to San Diego. Now get your crap and get on the next flight home."

Sedgewick turned on his heel and slammed open the swinging door and stormed out. Derek laughed, thinking how bad it would have been had someone been on the other side of the door at that moment. He shocked himself, wondering how he could be laughing as his career tanked. Yes, he *was* losing it.

On the flight home Derek's stomach rolled. He sipped club soda and wondered if he'd have a job when he got home. He wondered what Nina would say and then quickly decided he wouldn't tell her. As the plane made its descent, it hit turbulence in each cloud layer. They emerged into a rare rainy day in San Diego, which fit his mood perfectly. He watched Balboa Park slide through his rain-streaked window on final approach.

Derek came home to an empty house. He figured Nina and the girls were out running errands. He went upstairs to the bedroom and dropped his bags. He sat on the edge of the bed, squinting at the gray light coming through the blinds and felt like crying or screaming. He thought of the jug of vodka downstairs, in the cabinet above the refrigerator. He thought of the .357 Magnum he kept on the top shelf of the closet and where he had put the ammo. For the life of him, he'd no idea where he put the box of shells. He hadn't been able to find it for months and was too embarrassed to tell Nina he'd lost the bullets. God, he had to do something, anything, to get off this line of thinking or something terrible might happen.

Some strange and powerful drive led Derek as he changed into shorts and a t-shirt and then dug through the closet for his old sneakers. They looked pathetic. He grumbled profanity at the relics as he laced them up and took off through the front door, not understanding what he was doing or where he was headed. He only knew he had to get out and run. *Somewhere. Now.*

As he shuffled along the edge of the road he hoped maybe he'd get hit by a car or he'd have a heart attack. That way he wouldn't have to deal with the mess he'd made. Fate was not merciful. Instead, Derek slogged along the roadside, hearing the water slap with each footfall. It wasn't long before his lungs burned and his knees were grinding in protest. Occasionally a car would charge through a puddle, drenching him with dirty water. Strangely, this all seemed fair to Derek. Deserved. It was self-flagellation. Perhaps penance.

The run was an act of pure desperation. But even in the jarring process, calm came over him as he panted for precious oxygen. Maybe through running he could trade emotional pain for the physical kind. Derek finally saw his house coming back into view. He'd only run around the block, but it seemed like the Bataan Death March. As he walked through the front door, soaked and sore, Nina and the girls looked up in surprise.

"Hi Honey," Nina said as she and Bailey put away groceries. "We didn't expect you home until tomorrow." Hannah ran to him and threw her arms around his wet legs. "What were you doing?" Nina asked, setting the milk down to finally give Derek a good inspection. "Were you walking in this?"

Derek nodded.

"How did the meeting go?" Nina asked casually as she handed Bailey a bag of lettuce.

"Fine," Derek answered quickly. "We just finished early." The sting of lying to Nina in front of the kids lingered as he went up to shower.

The next day at work, Derek looked like he was headed to the gallows as he walked down the hall. When he'd opened his e-mail moments before, the first one was a curt note from Sedgewick that read *"See me now."* He had written off trying to excuse his frantic behavior in Houston, so instead his mind grasped for ways to tell Nina he was unemployed.

"Come," Sedgewick answered after the knock. Derek sheepishly walked into the office and sat down. Sedgewick made a steeple with his fingers as he leaned back in his chair, ever the caring coach.

"Derek, I've been rolling this over in my mind and based on your past years, I'm offering you one last shot to be part of this team." Derek was stunned. But before he had the chance to thank him, Sedgewick put up his hand and added acid to the offer.

"You'll be taking our rural clients."

Derek knew he was being demoted, but it all made sense now. Sedgewick had been looking for someone to take this slot, selling to rural clinics and Indian reservations. Sedgewick always pictured Derek as a good fit since he'd grown up in a small town and was Indian, but he didn't want to insult him with the lower commissions and remote travels. They both knew Derek would have to either take it or walk.

Derek reluctantly asked, "What about my other accounts? Houston, L.A., Las Vegas ..."

"We've got 'em all redistributed already."

Derek's blood drained from his face. All those years of networking, building relationships and establishing strong accounts in those bountiful environments. For what? The cash cow he'd built was being torn apart by a pack of vultures, benefiting from his years of hard work.

After the meeting, Derek went to the break room for coffee and ran into Skip.

"How you doing, Derek?" Skip asked, genuinely concerned.

"What did you get?"

Skip looked away. "Houston area."

"Good. At least you got that instead of Talbot or Menendez."

"Listen, I know this sucks Derek. But, for what it's worth, Sedgewick looked sad when he gave these new territories out." Derek glared at Skip. "I meant *your* territories."

"Well, I guess it's fitting to look sad at what amounts to a funeral for someone's career," Derek said. Tired and beaten, he knew he'd be on the worst sales circuit in the company and there wasn't a damn thing he could do about it.

Over the next week, Derek put on his sneakers and shuffled along the sidewalk through most of his lunch hour. He was too stressed to eat and he couldn't stand to sit in the office for his lunch break. Frustration at his predicament would build and so would the guilt of not telling Nina. So instead, he put on his shorts, t-shirt and pathetic shoes and tried to run. This was his punishment and his escape.

Each day was a new experiment in pain. His knees creaked, his hips cracked and his back shuddered. His lungs were on fire and side stitches exploded. His head throbbed. Soreness attacked places he didn't know existed. He had blisters on his feet and got an ingrown toenail. But despite the pain and discomfort, each day, Derek went a little farther and had to admit he felt calmer and less angry after each session. And running was much cheaper and less invasive than therapy.

It had been just over a week since the demotion. Derek opened his blinds and frowned at the pouring rain. He grabbed his gear and headed for the corporate fitness center. He didn't like the place, seeing it as an extension of work where yet another form of competition was promoted—showing off. Here he could see Sedgewick in a sweaty t-shirt and tight shorts, slapping backs and giving others unsolicited fitness tips. He could see the guy from the mailroom singing with his headphones or the jerk in the finance department banging big weights and glaring at everyone. The place was a potent cocktail of sweat, ego and attitude. Derek had been trying to keep his new activity to himself, but showing up here, he knew the word would be out—fat Derek is trying to get in shape.

As he checked in and got issued a hand towel, Derek received a surprised smile and a thumbs up from Skip while he got in his daily bike and flirt session. When Sedgewick grinned in approval and started to walk over, surely to coach him, Derek nearly left. He was saved when Gina from tech support grabbed Sedgewick for a question. Derek meekly climbed onto the treadmill and tried to manipulate a panel of controls that looked like it belonged on the flight deck of the starship *Enterprise*.

Once he was finally underway, he got into a clumsy but comfortable rhythm. He hit the up arrow to increase the speed. Sweat rolled down his head and he relaxed, listening to the hypnotic whir of the machinery. He hit the up arrow again. As his muscles loosened, the shuffle slowly transformed into something resembling a run. Derek started to feel a flutter in his stomach, a buzz. He winked at Skip and even gave a nod to Sedgewick. One of the fluorescent lights above him flickered, flared brightly, and then went out. Derek was oblivious, lost in the pleasant sensations.

Suddenly he felt light on his feet, too light, and he stumbled. With a loud squeak from his shoe rubbing the spinning belt, Derek crashed in a heap at the rear of the treadmill but not before getting a nasty belt burn on his knee as he did. The woman running on the treadmill next to him hit the emergency off button on Derek's machine. He slowly stood up, embarrassed and hurt as the belt slowed down. Everyone had stopped moving and the gym was eerily quiet. Some looked concerned and some looked amused, but they all looked at him. Skip hopped off his bike to walk over but Derek quickly darted out of the center before anyone could talk to him.

He cursed under his breath as he dabbed water onto his wound in the men's room. He gritted his teeth in frustration, wondering what he'd been thinking in the first place. Did he really think this was going to help him with his problems? His weight? His loss? He felt foolish, now believing he was too old and too fat to be taking up this hobby, and sure he'd be the brunt of any office party jokes from now until forever. Why was he going through all this pain when comfort could be found in the local liquor store? Or the closest fast food drive-thru? *Screw running* he thought as he changed his clothes and roughly jammed his gear into his bag. *I'm done with this horseshit!*

Derek walked in from work to find Nina sitting quietly at the kitchen table. In her hand, she held airline tickets.

"What are these?" she demanded. "I thought you were going to Las Vegas this week, not ..." she looked down to read the destination again, "not Pendleton, Oregon. What's going on, Derek?"

Derek bit his lip and looked down, knowing he was busted. "We've had a change in assignments at work."

"What kind of change? Skip never mentioned it and he always talks about work." Nina's expectant stare was too much to handle.

"Alright, *I've* had a change happen at work," Derek said. "Something happened in Houston." He paused to make sure he spun this right. "I've been transferred to our rural clients. Sedgewick thought this would be a good ..."

"Derek, when were you going to tell me this?" Nina looked betrayed. "This is definitely going to affect our income and with both girls in ballet now ..."

"Is that all this is about? Money?" Derek took the moment to feel justified in his anger, focusing on the money issue and not the fact that he'd lied to Nina and lost his accounts. "I work my ass off for this family! This is the thanks I get?"

Nina looked as if Derek had slapped her.

She took a deep breath and slowly continued, "I was *going to say* that I can go back to work if we need me to."

Derek felt cornered. Nina took away his line of argument with her comment. He was wrong and he knew it. Pride and anger wrapped around his throat.

"Please, Derek, just talk to me," Nina implored. "We're in this together, as a family."

Derek responded with silence.

"Damn it, Derek, talk to me before it's too late!" Nina's fierce effort to get a response was out of character, but it worked.

"Are you threatening me?" Derek scowled at her. "It's not enough I'm going through all this and now you're threatening divorce?" Derek was indignant and threw one final, flippant blow, "You know I guess I expected this to come up sooner or later."

"Derek, I'm just saying we need to work this out."

The words fell on deaf ears as Derek turned away from her and headed upstairs. Nina sat at the table staring numbly at the tickets, the betrayal incarnate.

A few moments later, Derek came stomping down the stairs wearing his running gear. As he headed through the front door, Nina asked where he was going and he tuned out her words, slamming the door behind him. With a deep breath, he lowered his head and started running. With each step on the concrete sidewalk, his rage pulsed. He ran past neighborhood houses glowering at those inside, hating them for their happiness. He cut through traffic, not waiting for the crossing signal, and defiantly ran amongst the honking horns while he threw up his middle finger.

Derek came closer to the edge of his neighborhood and gasped for air. But he couldn't stop. He wouldn't stop. His lungs screamed and his heart revolted as he hit a dirt trail by the park. He ran with rage. He ran away from regret, his guilt and his mistakes. He ran away from Nina, Hannah and Bailey. He ran from his life. Chest heaving, Derek's sweat poured and he grimaced as the scab on his knee split open. A shell was breaking away. He ran faster, harder. He thought of Cole.

With each footfall, he pictured a memory that would never be. He imagined tucking Cole in at night, reading him stories as he had with the girls. He imagined them fishing together. He imagined giving his son what he had missed out on as a little boy. Derek shook his head to erase the images.

He visualized each fall of his foot smashing into the face of the doctors, the parents who took their children home. He ran faster, smashing the faces of Sedgewick and those that stole his accounts. He clenched his fists, smashing his feet into the images of kids he grew up with in Oklahoma, his parents who left him behind. And he smashed God with his angry feet for all of it. But again, he came back to Cole.

As his feet hit the pavement in rhythm with his heart, Derek's mind started to calm. A picture of Cole, perfect and still and wearing a blue knit cap floated into Derek's mind. His heart ached for this boy he could fit in his hand. A state of synchronicity embraced him like a soft blanket. He'd pushed through the pain and now enjoyed his second wind and the classic runner's high. Derek dreamily looked up as a streetlight flared brightly and then went dark. He felt like laughing, crying and yelling all at once. He was euphoric. Then, all of a sudden his wave of good feelings was replaced by waves of nausea. Derek slowed his run to a jog and then to a trot. Finally, he walked to the side of the road and promptly threw up.

Standing up after a few heaves, Derek wiped his mouth. *No pain, no gain* he sardonically thought as he leaned over, bracing his arms on his knees. He saw crimson streaks from his cracked open scab running into his sock. He managed a smile, feeling better and enjoying the post run high, despite the vomiting.

The phone rang for the third time and Nina's heart raced, torn between making this call and doing nothing.

On the other end of the line, the phone tweeted loudly in its cradle. Martha Sorensen grimaced in pain, holding her hip as she limped toward it. Don was supposed to set up that answering machine for moments like this, but she knew he was as confused by the equipment and its set up as she was. With this change in the weather, walking had been more uncomfortable than usual, and getting anywhere quickly was excruciating. Wincing, she grabbed the phone on the fifth ring to no avail. The line was already dead.

CHAPTER 4

NINA ROLLED OVER and stared at Derek lying uncov-
ered beside her in bed. She could see the scrapes on his hands and
the ghastly scab on his knee and was tempted to feel sorry for him.
He seemed so vulnerable, sleeping soundly in his patterned boxer
shorts.

Though Derek had gotten heavier and aged noticeably in the
last year, she was still strongly attracted to him. She looked longingly at his short, scrubby black hair and his handsome rugged
features. She wanted to touch his face but stayed her hand. She
didn't want to disturb him, this man in the bed that had become a
stranger to her. How had it come to this?

Nina had met Derek on a windy day on Coronado Island in
San Diego. Derek saw her shopping at an outdoor rack of swim-
suits as he left a restaurant. He later admitted to her that though
normally shy with women, he was drawn to her like the tides to the
moon.

"That will never fit you," he'd said in a clumsy attempt to be
funny.

"Well it sure as heck won't fit you either!" she'd replied.

Nina's long hair kept blowing in her face like an attacking
octopus as she tried to talk with him, making them both laugh. In

even the short exchange, Derek reminded her of her dad with his quiet charisma and gentle nature.

Nina's dad was a son of an Iowa farmer. He'd been a serviceman stationed in Okinawa when he met her mom in the 1960s. Quite the odd couple, her dad had curly light brown hair, stood over six feet tall and had green eyes. Her mom was barely five feet tall and Japanese. Her dad was quiet and steady and her mom bubbled with energy. Love was truly blind for the two and easily bridged the differences. Her dad had joined the military to find adventures far from the farm, and he surely found it in her. He took Keiko back to the U.S. where they were married. She was only 18 and he was 19.

Keiko embraced the American lifestyle quickly, seeming to have been meant for it all along. She already knew how to speak English from the schools in Okinawa, but decided to go to college and get her degree in teaching. In the process, Keiko dropped the "ko" from her name and since Kei was pronounced *Kay* anyway, the transition to an Americanized name was complete. Nina was born shortly after and the three of them lived happily at March Air Force base in Riverside, California.

When Nina was only seven years old, her dad was diagnosed with cancer. Just after Christmas of her eighth year, her dad died, leaving her and her mom alone. It was then that her mom started calling her *Sakura*, or cherry blossom, that beautifully delicate but hardy flower that emerged each spring no matter how hard or terrible the winter had been.

Nina's marriage to Derek for the past ten years had been filled with love, happy memories and stability. But it seemed that with the loss of Cole, something broke inside Derek, a dam had given way and Nina couldn't figure out how to help him put it back together. She often wondered if he harbored a secret anger at her for the baby's loss. Nina could only guess through the quiet between them.

Though he lay a few inches from her in bed, Derek seemed thousands of miles away from her. She wondered what he dreamed. She wondered how to keep the family together. Especially after witnessing the impact of a family ripped apart, she refused to let this occur for the sake of the girls, even though it seemed Derek was almost willing this to happen. She wanted to work this out and help Derek in any way she could. Her mind drifted to Hannah and Bailey.

Bailey was so much like Derek, the good and the bad. She got his independence, smarts and quiet resolve but also his stubbornness and tendency to withdraw within. Bailey and Derek's special bond began on the day she was born. After attending a ten-week natural childbirth class together, Derek was allowed to deliver her. His hands were the first to touch her in this world and it was if he'd anointed her with his foibles and strengths in the process.

Though Hannah was more like Nina, outgoing and cheerful, she wanted to be just like her daddy. It made Nina concerned that Derek seemed strange around the kids anymore. He went from the gentle guiding hand trying to be the best dad he could be to an emotionally absent father. He often came across as impatient or merely distant, but sometimes even appeared skittish to be around them.

Nina rubbed her eyes and wistfully grinned, thinking of Derek's slight southern drawl that only made an appearance when he was tired or had been drinking. She knew he'd made a conscious effort to lose it when he left Oklahoma, though she never understood why. She thought it was charming.

Her thoughts always made it full circle, back to the one that mattered most, "What is happening to this family?" Didn't their love, their relationship, this family mean anything to Derek? She knew he took Cole's loss harder than anyone, but his crisis now gnawed away at the family like a pack of hungry rats.

Nina knew she wasn't over Cole's loss either. The pain of a mother losing a child was like a nightmare from which she never would fully wake. But she steadily, consciously, was dealing with the anguish and trying to reassemble the pieces left in the wake of the loss.

When it first happened, Nina feared she was going crazy. She had panic attacks while out in public with the girls, thinking she might be dying of a heart attack or having a stroke. She often cried herself to sleep at night and filled her and the girls' days with activity to keep from thinking about Cole, all the while replaying what she might have done to cause his premature birth. Nina knew what she needed to do as an expectant mother after having Bailey and Hannah. She'd followed the doctor's orders exactly, hadn't she?

One day when Derek was traveling and the girls were at school, Nina had taken out the baby's cap, gown and blanket, arranged them as if he were wearing them and cradled them in her arms. She crumpled into a sobbing heap on the floor. That was the day she knew she needed help and wasn't too proud to admit it. Nina knew Derek was in his own dark wilderness, unwilling to communicate or even start a road to recovery so she took matters into her own hands.

Nina relied heavily on talks with her mom and her closest friends. She'd joined the church they'd previously only attended on Christmas and Easter. She joined a support group for women who'd lost babies and read every book she could get her hands on about dealing with loss. Derek would have none of it. She'd gone back to journaling, something she'd loved but gave up after the girls were born. Her one-time hobby became a healing refuge, a supportive friend and therapist. Nina believed fervently that she would one day hold her baby again in heaven.

She wasn't over the loss of Cole but actively worked toward healing and to put the loss into perspective. She couldn't recover what was gone but wanted to be there for the family she still had. Staring hopefully at Derek, she tried to reach out to him with her mind and heart. Finally she rolled over and faded off to sleep.

Derek got up before the alarm went off. His sleep had been restless and his mind disturbed. He decided to take a short run before work. He grabbed his gear and changed in the dark, looking down at Nina.

He wondered if they'd ever make love again. It had been so long already and he knew he'd been the reason. He'd resisted her even though he knew it hurt them both to do so. Though he ached for her, he couldn't open up that way to her and instead feigned tiredness or drew on his anger to avoid the romance. He reached down and traced her shoulder with his finger, letting it play amongst her hair. He'd always been fascinated with Nina's exotic beauty, having the delicate Asian features but with unique green eyes. Her skin was clear as sky save the spate of light freckles across her upper cheeks and the bridge of her nose. These features, along with her personality, made her seem eternally youthful and sprite-like.

When they were dating, Derek knew Nina was told she was beautiful all her life, so he playfully teased instead, saying beauty back where he grew up meant you had all your teeth.

Derek stood up and sighed. His love for Nina felt like dying of thirst in a glass-bottomed boat. He could see what he wanted, what he desperately needed, but Derek just couldn't, for some reason, get through that final inch of glass. He turned and left the room.

A few minutes into the run, he hit his stride. The cool morning air crawled along his sweaty neck and he looked down at his watch. As his feet tapped the asphalt, he gazed at his distorted shadow bobbing in the orange light of the streetlamps. He could see a ribbon of deep crimson along the horizon, heralding the rise of the sun. One of the amber lights above him began to waver wildly and emanate a growing hum that reached crescendo as he passed below it. The orb of glass shattered in a shower of purple and white sparks and he deftly avoided the falling shards as they tinkled onto the asphalt. Derek reflected on the timing of such an event. *What are the odds?*

As Derek continued, a tingling sensation grew in his stomach and chest. It trickled down his legs and into his feet. It felt like he waded up to his armpits in liquid electricity as he ran. As he considered what was happening, he got distracted by the hotspot he was getting on his big toe again. *I've got to get new shoes* Derek thought as the tingling faded.

Later that day, during his lunch break, Derek decided to hit the sporting goods store around the corner, hoping he wouldn't see anyone he knew. He found the running department and perused the vast selection of shoes on the wall. After a few minutes the sheer magnitude of options overwhelmed him. He'd had the same sneakers for over a decade and in that time shoes had gone through a revolution. The wild colors, designs, descriptions and technology made him just stare blankly until he saw the price tags. Then he grunted and rolled his eyes.

"Can I help you, sir?" a salesman asked Derek. He must have been in his late forties, but the man looked like a weathered leathery version of a teenage athlete. His wiry legs and arms were laced with thick, ropy blue veins running throughout. The man's head, topped with a large, wild bush of chestnut hair, sealed the adolescent look.

"I'm just looking for some new running shoes."

"Well, alright," the salesman said, genuinely happy. "I'm Harvey and I'll be able to help you with that, dude."

The guy seemed to talk too slow and to be too happy to be sober. As the two looked at the shoes, Harvey asked Derek about his fitness goals, running experience and any health or foot issues he may have. He put Derek on a treadmill and analyzed with a video camera the way his foot fell. Derek waited to next be asked for a DNA sample. Or urine.

After they found the right shoes, Harvey tried to interest Derek in silky, high-cut shorts he wouldn't have worn at home alone in the bathtub. He tried to explain how the silky tank top he showed him would keep his nipples from getting chaffed and how Nalgene sport bottles would keep his water from tasting like liquid plastic.

Derek shook his head at each offer. "I just want the shoes."

Harvey lovingly patted the box after he'd put the shoes back into it.

"Yeah, you're right man. These babies are all you really need anyway."

"How long have you been running?" Derek asked as he counted out the cash.

"Since the seventies," Harvey said with a widening smile. "I was trying to trip out with chemicals back then and running became part of my recovery. After awhile, I found I didn't need all that other stuff to feel high anymore. I got what I needed in the running."

"You mean a runner's high?"

"No man, way beyond," Harvey said as he looked for the right word. "It's ... spiritual."

For a moment Harvey seemed to be in his own world, looking out into some faraway place. "You feel reconnected. Just put one foot in front of the other and life becomes simple again, pure."

"Sounds good," Derek said and laid the cash on the counter.

The clerk shook his head back and forth to clear away the ether and smiled. "I have to say I'm truly excited for you, dude," he said. "You'll see what I mean."

The next day at lunch, Derek went through his usual routine of grabbing his gear to change. But when he opened his gym bag, his heart raced as he smelled the scent of new shoes. As he laced them up, he remembered last night.

He'd called Nina to tell her he'd be working late. But when he got home earlier than expected, he found the house empty—again. Nina's disappearing act was increasingly frequent and it had Derek worried. *What was she doing? Where was she going?* The kids were always at Kay's, but Nina was vague with her too. Derek stopped his mind from going down this stygian tunnel and refocused on the run.

He decided to try his new shoes out for a run on Coronado Beach. The beach was wide and flat, hard packed with the black sand and golden flecks that made Coronado famous. The drive was quiet, being midday and not tourist season. As he drove across the enormous blue steel curve that formed Coronado Bridge, Derek's mind went back to Nina, the only woman he'd ever loved. She was the only person in his life he could open up to and even then, not completely. He continued to carry the guilt of that deception.

Nina was Derek's port in the storm, his only peace and safe harbor. Though he'd been doing a terrible job of showing it, he desperately needed her. Nina seemed the last bastion of hope for his healing from Cole's loss and he wondered if soon, she'd be leaving him too. Derek grew frustrated and cynical as his jaw muscles tightened. *It would be typical* he acidly thought, reflecting on a life of disappointments and let downs.

Even during their courtship, it was Nina's patience and persistence that had coaxed Derek's heart out into the open. Everyone has parts of their inner self they keep private, but Derek's territory was vast. Though he let kingdom after kingdom fall to Nina in time, they did not surrender easily or completely.

Derek parked the car and hit the beach, starting off with a gentle trot to get a feel for the new shoes. They felt good. He felt good. He kicked up his pace and enjoyed the stiff breeze coming off the ocean and the welcome absence of other people. The hypnotic hiss of the waves spilling onto the beach was interrupted by the whining roar of a Navy fighter jet, an F-18 Hornet, with its distinctly angled twin tails. It spit ghostly contrails from its wingtips. After several minutes, he opened his stride, imagining himself as the F-18, and the tingling sensation returned. It wasn't pins and needles, but like a low-voltage current running under his skin in all directions. As Derek ran, the sensation strengthened and spread to his limbs. He enjoyed the beginnings of euphoria. *Maybe this is what Harvey was talking about.*

Suddenly he no longer sensed the ground beneath his feet. It seemed like the wind lifted him up like the homemade kites he used to fly in Oklahoma as a kid. Without warning he fell with a face-plant on the hard packed sand. "Son of a bitch!" he shouted in fury as he stood up and hopped up and down in pain. The scab on his knee had been sheared off and sat on the sand looking like a giant burgundy corn flake. Derek paced around in a circle, cursing loudly and brushing sand off his clothes. He tenderly tried to rub the sand away from the edges of the fresh wound that was no longer protected. Instead, the gummy area acted like a magnet, attracting every grain of sand Derek tried to flick away. *Why the hell did this keep happening?*

As he paced around, catching his breath between profanities, he looked at his footprints. He traced them backward to just before he stumbled. What he saw just didn't make sense. It couldn't. Derek looked down and saw a span of fifteen or twenty feet with no footprints. The distinct and deep waffle pattern of his new shoes was hard to miss, but Derek kept looking. *Did the tide wash away the prints?* No, he was at least fifty feet from the water's edge. As he inspected the ground, Derek thought perhaps he'd tripped and flown the distance. After measuring the distance several times, he realized the impossibility of that.

His curiosity shifted from the mystery of the disappearing footprints to the strange cause of the weird sensations and his frequent falls. Worried, he decided to make an appointment with an old friend and client, Dr. Fred Parker. In the meantime, Derek decided to soothe his frustration with a double cheeseburger and a couple beers at *Hang Ten Bar and Grill*.

Derek's jaunt to *Hang Ten* became a ravenous but forlorn gorging session. Jamming the fatty, greasy food into his mouth was yet another attempt to satiate the hunger that had little to do with food at all. The couple beers became many and the imbibing included an arsenal of shots to seal the checked-out feeling he'd wanted. It had worked so well, Derek barely remembered getting tossed from the restaurant and having a taxi called for him in lieu of the police.

Even in his drunken state, Derek had the good sense to sleep on the couch. Nina knew what had happened—guessing hadn't been needed in the equation for quite some time. She kept the girls away from him and occupied as they got ready for school. He couldn't see her face but imagined Nina's expression: a mix of sadness and anger, but hopefully tempered with a gratitude he'd made it home. Or did she even care anymore? Derek knew he'd done this too many times to be worthy of anything but disgust. Even he was disgusted.

Derek felt like a leper and knew he must have smelled like a back alley. The liquor and greasy food had conspired in his stomach to create a noxious bubbling cauldron of regret. His throat burned from reflux and he had some kind of greasy maroon sauce down the front of his shirt. Where the hell were his pants? Derek gingerly lifted one eyelid to the world around him just as the door slammed, aggravating a throbbing head. He knew he'd be late for work again. Derek extricated himself from the San Diego Chargers blanket which had wrapped him up like a fuzzy straight jacket. He got up and stumbled to the bathroom and almost made it before he stepped on a Barbie doll and her hard plastic accessories. It was like stepping on a pit of punji stakes. Derek hobbled the rest of the way, cursing under his breath, knowing he deserved it.

"So how's the family doing, Derek?" Dr. Parker asked as he examined Derek's chart through small reading glasses.

"Oh, they're fine," Derek said automatically. He sat on the exam table looking around and letting his legs dangle like a kid. The paper gown he wore made him seem even more ridiculous.

What was left of Dr. Parker's hair had formed a snowy ring around the back of his dark brown head. He had been one of the first black doctor's to graduate from any college in Mississippi back in the sixties. He'd earned every one of those white hairs.

"We sure loved that banana bread Nina made for us during the holidays," Dr. Parker said warmly as he rubbed his belly. "The Misses got on me for wolfing down most of it."

Derek nervously watched Dr. Parker flip through the chart. "How'd that scanner work out for you?" Derek asked, pointing to the ultrasound machine in the corner.

"It's fine now after you made those probe changes for our new tech," Dr. Parker said absently. "He tried to do a heart scan with a vaginal probe."

He looked at Derek over the top of his glasses and they both laughed.

"Well, at Global Medix we aim to please," Derek said.

"So how long have you been running?" Dr. Parker asked.

"Only about four weeks."

"Well what you're doing seems to be working. Not only is your blood pressure down, but you've lost seven pounds and lowered your resting heart rate," Dr. Parker noted.

"Really?" Derek asked, genuinely surprised.

"Derek, have you ever had a spinal cord injury?" Dr. Parker asked as he sat down.

Derek shook his head.

"Not that I know of."

"I'm just wondering what could be giving these symptoms. You say you're feeling, what's the word you used here ... electricity. Well, that's a typical sensation for a nervous system on the fritz, like from pinched nerves. Any pain?"

"No, no pain. Actually, it's just the opposite. It feels good, like my blood is buzzing. It feels like I'm floating. Well, it feels good until I trip and fall."

Dr. Parker looked concerned and took off his glasses.

"I'm going to recommend some X-rays and an MRI to see if we can figure this out. Talk to Michelle on the way out to get scheduled, okay?"

Derek nodded. The two casually chatted as Dr. Parker wrote up the orders but neither of them felt closer to an answer after the exam.

Skip had been noticing Derek's melancholy and asked him out for a drink after work. Derek reluctantly agreed, not really wanting to share his issues with anyone. But on the other hand, it was eating away at him. Maybe a drink wouldn't be such a bad idea after all.

They went to a swanky upscale martini bar in the historic Gas Lamp District of downtown San Diego. They grabbed a quiet table in the back. Derek ordered a beer and Skip got a fruity neon green martini that resembled anti-freeze.

"I'm sure you're wondering why I called this meeting today," Skip said playfully as he did his best impression of Sedgewick.

Derek grinned.

"Seriously though, how've you been doing lately?" The two talked about the weather, football and work, and a few drinks later Derek relaxed.

Derek kept most people at a safe distance, which prevented him from having many close friends, but Skip was his best. Derek was often seen as aloof or withdrawn, but he was cautious about trusting people and it took more time than most cared to invest. But since Skip and Derek had worked together for so long, trust had taken root. Though reluctant to talk, the pressure inside Derek had been building and the beer loosened the hinges. The truth seemed less intimidating through intoxicated eyes.

"I think Nina's thinking of leaving," Derek said looking intently at his beer as if it held the answers.

"Where's she going?" Skip asked and casually sipped his strange concoction.

"Leaving *me*," Derek clarified with annoyance.

"Come on, Derek," Skip protested, waving his hand at the thought. "Nina and you are like peanut butter and jelly. I know you two have had a rough year, but she's not going anywhere."

Derek didn't look so sure. "She's been disappearing nights, leaving the kids at her mom's." Derek felt bare now that the words spilled out.

Skip's lukewarm look was no solace.

"You guys want another round?" the heavily tattooed waitress asked, only looking at Skip. She'd been flirting with him since they were seated but all her facial piercings were unsettling.

"Sure, why not?" Skip replied, not looking up.

Derek nodded and used the distraction to shift gears and talk about work. He'd been frustrated with his new assignments. Derek also told Skip that he'd been reflecting about Cole's loss and his own life, surprised by his own candor. He even tried to explain the sensations and experiences he'd been having on his runs.

On the way home, Derek regretted how open he'd been with Skip. He'd never been one to share his fears or deep feelings with anyone and now he felt vulnerable. But the conversation had also given some relief, like letting a bit of air out of a swollen balloon. He wondered if he could do the same with Nina. But when he got home, everyone was asleep. Derek hadn't realized how late it had gotten and quietly crawled into bed. Looking at the clock, he sighed. He knew he'd only get a few hours of sleep before he had to get to the airport. He was headed for South Dakota ... and for changes he never saw coming nor could have imagined.

As the small plane came in for a landing, Derek saw an ocean of rolling hills and prairie. Wide open and empty, it seemed barren and lonely to Derek. The wheels screeched and the airplane shuddered as it rolled to a stop. Derek looked at the facility and doubted it was big enough to even qualify as an airport. He got a rental car and drove to his tiny motel that would be home for the next two days. As he unpacked, his cell phone went off and Derek hoped it was Nina. It was Dr. Parker.

"Derek?" the crackling voice sounded like it came from a distant planet. "I called to follow up with you since you forgot to talk to Michelle and come in for those tests. We need to square this away when you get back."

"Okay, Fred, will do," Derek said but had no intention of doing so.

"Oh, and I forgot to tell you to go ahead and keep running. It looks like it's reaping some great benefits for you."

"Sounds good. Thanks," Derek added before ending the call. With that bit of encouragement, Derek decided to go explore and unwind with a run.

As Derek ran through the town, he spied a small diner with floral curtains, a purple neon "OPEN" sign with only the letters E and N lit. The white-washed gas station was ancient, had only two manual pumps, and no credit card swiping or digital displays. The paint was flaking terribly and the crowded window advertised everything from hunting licenses, Skoal and lotto tickets to faded out-of-date sales banners for STP, Valvoline and the goofy cartoon turtle promoting Turtle Wax. Mud-splattered pickups passed with billowy eagle plumes hanging from the rearview mirror. And none of them looked like they'd ever used Turtle Wax.

He watched the people in the community, mostly Native American, wave at each other and to him. With his brown skin and black hair, he looked like them but felt like a foreigner. Knots of lingering kids were everywhere and Derek watched one group alternately chase and then be chased by a pair of mangy dogs. It wasn't quite Norman Rockwell but it was far removed from the suburban life he lived for so long.

Feeling out of sorts from travel, Derek cut his run short and jogged to a small grocery store. He walked in circles near the entrance, nursing a side stitch with his hand.

"You know if you put your hands on top of your head, that will help," a voice said from behind a tribal newspaper.

"Thanks," Derek said between breaths.

"You running *to* something or *from* something?" the voice asked.

The question caught Derek off guard and then the joke dawned on him. "Oh, right. No, I'm just running."

"You a skin?" the man said, lowering his paper.

"Huh?" Derek was confused.

"Are you a skin?" The man saw the question didn't register in Derek. "A redskin. You Indian?"

"Yeah, I am." Derek looked down at his arms and body as if to reconfirm it for himself. "But I was adopted and don't know what tribe I'm from."

The man seemed unimpressed and muttered "toka hokshila" as he leaned back against the front of the store in his fold up lawn chair. He wore dusty cowboy boots and Wrangler jeans topped with a large belt buckle tucked slightly under a bowling ball belly hidden beneath a plaid, button up shirt. His long, salt-and-pepper hair in two braids hung from under a large black Stetson. He looked like an aged Indian version of the Marlboro Man. He rocked the chair forward, stood up on bowed legs and reached out his hand.

"Arnold Kills Straight. Welcome to Deer Creek."

"Thank you," Derek said. "I'm Derek Sorensen. Nice to meet you."

Derek wiped the sweat off his hand and reached out to Arnold's. The man had broad shoulders, a barrel chest and strong arms, but shook Derek's hand in a firm but gentle way, with one pump. How different the handshake was from Sedgewick's crushing squeeze and cranking action, like he was pumping a well and dying of thirst. Arnold's weathered brown face had a long scar under his left eye that looked like a teardrop had cut a furrow on the way down.

Derek told Arnold he was in town selling medical equipment and asked for directions to the Indian Health Clinic.

"You must be the fella Sarah mentioned. She's a nurse administrator over at the clinic."

A woman with an overcoat, orthopedic shoes and twinkling eyes came out of the store and pinched the back of Arnold's arm.

"Ouch!" Arnold rubbed the spot with a grin. "Derek, this is my wife Ruby." She smiled warmly at Derek and nodded her head. "He's here to work with Sarah over at the clinic," Arnold said to his wife. "Toka hokshila."

"You look like you're gonna fall over. You should come to the house and have some stew with us," Ruby said.

The kindness of the invitation caught Derek by surprise. "Thank you, but I really can't. I've got a ton of paperwork to get through tonight."

"Well, maybe next time," she said and grabbed the keys off Arnolds pocket chain. "Hokshila waste he," she said to Arnold and walked back to the truck.

"What did she say?" Derek asked.

"He's a nice boy," Arnold translated.

"Thanks, Arnold," Derek said. "It was good meeting you and your wife. Hopefully I'll see you again."

Arnold grinned. "I'm pretty sure we're gonna meet again, Kola. Take care." He turned and pretended to chase his wife as she giggled.

On the drive home Ruby filed her nails with a broken piece of Emory board and noticed Arnold's jaw flexing, showing he was deep in thought.

"Mmm?" she asked as only a wife could.

"I don't know. I feel like I know that boy." Arnold squinted and scratched his cheek.

"I like him," Ruby offered and continued filing. "Maybe you met him somewhere before."

"Yeah, could be." Arnold said the words but didn't believe them. He'd only just met the man, but instantly connected to him, like they had always been meant to meet or had always known each other. Arnold grinned and tapped the steering wheel in time to the pow-wow mix tape playing in the truck. He had learned not to over analyze such deep sensations because what was simply was. The spirits had their reasons for the messages they sent and only through prayer and time could those be revealed.

The next day Derek got coffee at a diner next to the hotel. It tasted like battery acid and had grounds floating in it. The Styrofoam cup of the grog and a stale bagel were breakfast as he got in the rental car and headed for the clinic.

Once he arrived Derek hadn't gone ten feet past the sliding glass doors before he was stopped.

"You must be Mr. Sorensen," the woman said excitedly with a genuine glow. "We've been looking at your website and there are several pieces of equipment we'd like to talk to you about. I'm Sarah."

Derek shook her hand.

"Please, call me Derek."

"Okay, *Derek,* you got it," Sarah replied.

Derek guessed Sarah was in her early thirties. She was stunning though she wore no make up or jewelry. Her shiny black hair hung in a long single braid and her eyes looked like dollops of melted chocolate. She wore the big Croc clogs that many medical staff wore but hers were hot pink. He saw her name tag read *Sarah Pretty On Top, RN.* How well the name fit the person.

"We were happy to hear Global Medix was sending a Native rep down here. What tribe are you?" she asked as they walked down the hall together. Derek always disliked the question and he now realized he'd probably get it all the time. In San Diego, people often assumed he was Mexican and apart from the awkwardness of others speaking Spanish to him, he felt comfortable with the ambiguity. But here on reservations he'd be serving, he knew that time was over. Derek clumsily explained his status and Sarah seemed to empathize.

"Are you from here?" Derek asked.

"No. I'm Crow from Montana," she said, expecting a response from Derek. "You know, traditional enemy of the Lakota?"

Derek's face gave away his ignorance and Sarah shifted gears.

"Ah, just kidding anyway," Sarah said. "That was the old days."

They walked into the clinic's birthing center and both washed first with green anti-bacterial soap. The smell reminded him of each of the countless times he went into the NICU to be with Cole. As Derek stood at the sink with foamy hands, Sarah's smile and words swirled away along with the steady hum of fluorescent lights ...

Derek and Nina were quiet as they looked down at Cole with glistening eyes. It had been several days since the doctors shared the news with them, but today the conversation bore a crushing weight. The medical staff had talked to them about the choice, the surreal and gut wrenching choice, of continuing the fight to save Cole or letting him go in peace. On the bedside table sat a small carving given to them by Kay, an angel with wire wings clutching a baby boy in her arms.

The decision seemed like a sick joke from God, presented Monty Hall-style to the couple with the doctors playing announcers. Derek and Nina were in a state of paralysis with the decision, wanting to continue the fight to bring their precious child home despite the medical prognosis predicting death, severe brain damage or PVS (permanent vegetative state).

But looking down at their son, they saw a tiny boy struggling to live with a body not meant for this world, hooked to wires, needles, tubes, a breathing machine and now a chest tube put in last night. Could they live with a decision to continue the suffering and struggle Cole endured? Was it loving or selfish? Could they live with the decision to let him die peacefully? Was that loving or selfish? They talked around it but how could they decide something like this? How could they live with either choice they made? It ripped at their hearts like claws.

On the seventh day of Cole's life, Derek stepped out for awhile to get a cup of coffee and some fresh air. As he watched an airliner fly overheard, he wondered when he'd wake up from this nightmare. He threw his cup into the bin and headed back into the complex.

After scrubbing his hands, Derek entered the NICU and saw a flurry of activity centered on the rear of the NICU by Cole's crib. He quickened his pace. As he came around the last row of cribs, he saw Nina crying and holding Cole. She looked up at him like she'd broken a piece of China. Cole had extubated himself from life support, spitting out the tubes he needed for survival. Though too weak to move or even open his eyes, he managed this somehow and saved his parents from their heartbreaking conundrum. The nurses were trying to keep oxygen going to Cole with a handheld bag as the others quickly worked to reconnect the equipment, but his heart rate rapidly dropped. Derek fell to his knees beside Nina and they both held Cole as he grew pale.

Derek and Nina both knew what was happening to their son and shook their heads in unison to the nurses, wanting these final moments to be with them and not in the hands of others. The nurses seemed to breathe relief, knowing there was little they could do now anyway. Derek and Nina leaned in and whispered loving words to their baby.

"Shhh, it's okay, it's okay. We love you so much," Nina said while rocking gently.

Derek saw Cole's eyes open for the first time and said through tears, "We're here. It's okay, Cole. We love you. Just sleep Cole. It's okay." But inside Derek screamed, *Don't leave me. Please don't go, Cole! Please don't leave me!*

Cole's body twisted. He gasped. His eyes seemed to register not pain or fear, but surprise, as shocked as his parents were that he was leaving them. Suddenly, in the arms of his mommy and daddy, he went limp. His eyes slowly closed as the color faded from his skin. Their son was gone.

"Derek? Are you okay?" Sarah stared at him with concern.

Derek snapped out of his trance and realized he had tears running down his cheeks. Quickly wiping them away, he lied. "Sorry, it's just allergies. I'm fine."

The rest of the visit was a blur and Derek absentmindedly followed Sarah from room to room as she explained the clinic's needs. At the first moment that didn't seem like he was running away, he did, promising to follow up with Sarah later. She shook his hand and waved to him from the front door of the clinic. He wasn't supposed to be departing until tomorrow, but he had to leave. Now.

Derek's head swirled on his flight home. He felt weak and drained. The wounds had all been ripped open again. Why couldn't he move on from this tragic loss like everyone else had? He grew claustrophobic in the small cabin of the regional jet and ordered a drink. Then another. The balm acted on his head, but not his heart. Maybe the next one would.

Back home Nina watched a Disney movie with the girls when the phone rang.

"Hi Nina. It's Skip."

She paused, wondering if something had happened to Derek. Before she could ask, he continued.

"I had some drinks with Derek the other night and we talked. I'm sorry I kept him out so late, but he sounds really bad. I think he's starting to have a break down. He even talked about hallucinations he's been having. I wanted to come over and talk to you if that's okay."

Nina felt vindicated now that even Derek's best friend was seeing what she saw every day. Out of loyalty, she never shared their situation with anyone besides her mom. But Derek's decline seemed to be accelerating.

"Sure, Skip. Let me get the kids to bed. Give me about a half hour."

Skip came in and Nina offered him some peppermint tea she'd just put on. They small-talked awkwardly for a few minutes, neither of them knowing how to approach the subject. Nina held her cup in both hands, gripping it desperately. "So, tell me, how bad is it?"

The two talked for the better part of an hour, sharing their concerns, wondering about solutions and trying to make sense of it all. They were finishing up and Nina made a joke about Hannah's recent imitations of the evening news anchorman. In the middle of great laugh, the door flew open and startled them both.

Derek stood weaving in the doorway, looking sad and disheveled. He immediately fixed his bloodshot eyes at the two sharing a laugh at the kitchen table at this late hour as his drunken imagination ran wild.

"What the hell is this?" he asked with slurred speech, dropping his briefcase where he stood. His eyes narrowed. Nina stood up quickly.

"Oh, I see. It's all making sense now," Derek said. He tried to jerk his wedding ring off but it wouldn't budge from his fat finger. Nina looked nervous and Skip looked confused.

"What are you talking about Derek?" Skip shot back. "I just came over ..."

"No, no, I see," Derek quipped, scratching his head. "I get it now." Nina and Skip fell over themselves in explanation, now realizing how this might have looked to Derek.

"You always said you'd go for Nina if we got divorced and here you are Skip."

Skip looked at Nina with wide eyes and no time to explain the inside joke. He simply held his mouth open, wondering who to address.

Nina fired back, "Derek, this isn't what you think."

Derek lunged forward and grabbed Skip, lifting him to his feet. Skip's French blue shirt balled up in Derek's fists.

"First you take my territories and now you're trying to take my wife!" he hissed.

Nina screamed, "Derek, stop! What are you doing?"

"Is this who you've been disappearing with during the last month Nina, leaving our kids with your mother?" Derek growled as he glared murderously at Skip.

Skip looked straight into Derek's feral eyes.

"Listen to you, Derek! You sound like a madman—and you're drunk." Skip turned his head to catch a breath of air not laced with stink. "I'm your best friend and Nina loves you."

Derek refused to listen and tightened his grip on Skip's collar, breathing hard with the effort. Nina cried and Hannah and Bailey gawked through the banister at the scene.

To save the family from more of this awful scene, Skip cut to the quick.

"What you gonna do Derek, hit me?" Skip calmly asked.

The words seemed to fall like hammers on Derek, taking the fight out of him. He released his grip and looked ashamed as he stumbled backward.

Skip grabbed his keys and walked out without looking back. Nina shooed the girls back to bed, stuttering through sobs, and followed them upstairs. Derek stood there panting in the aftermath.

A few moments later Nina came back downstairs holding a large photo album covered in fancy paper.

"I can't believe you'd accuse me of ... what you were accusing me of, Derek!" Her voice still trembled through tears. "Do you really want to know what I've been doing, where I've been?" She thrust the large decorated book out in front of her. "I've been making this!"

Derek looked confused as Nina threw the album at the floor. It landed awkwardly, spilling the contents and landing with pages open and bent. At first Derek didn't seem to recognize the tangle of colorful papers and pictures, but then he looked stunned as he realized it was the pieces of their lives together. There were ticket stubs from their Hawaii trip, pictures of them when they were dating and pieces of art done by the girls. Pictures of their wedding, the girls as babies and family trips they'd enjoyed were spread on the ground.

Derek took a deep breath and looked ill.

"I made it for you, trying to remind you of what you have, *who* you have," Nina said, composing herself. "I guess it was a waste of time." She turned away and walked back upstairs.

Derek collapsed to his hands and knees, looking at the girls made up for Halloween and the picture of him and Nina kissing on a ski lift. He saw the countless creative details that Nina had added to the scrapbook, doodles with markers and construction paper frames. Derek saw all these magical memories, bent and in disarray over the kitchen floor. He fumbled through the papers, trying in vain to put the pieces of their lives back together.

CHAPTER 5

NINA PACED BACK and forth as she held the phone. After a deep breath and big sigh, she raised it and punched the numbers. After several rings, Nina heard a man's voice.

"Hullo?"

"Hi Don. It's Nina," she said as she nervously twisted a lock of hair.

Nina had convinced Derek to take the girls to the park and she saw this as the perfect time to call in backup on the situation. Nina usually had a keen insight to Derek, but Pappa Don was always willing to fill in the gaps. She needed some advice and support—and answers—more than ever.

"Nina, so good to hear from you darlin'. I was just getting Martha her pills and propping up her leg so she could watch *Price is Right*. I'd give the phone to her but it won't reach from here, so I'm afraid you're stuck with me," he said.

"That's fine, Don. I actually called to talk to you." The two talked for a few minutes about the girls and recent news. Don's honey-laced drawl always had a calming effect on Nina. She relaxed enough to bring up Derek. She explained what had been going on lately and was met with silence on the other end of the line. "Don, did you hear me?" Nina cautiously asked.

"I did. Nina, I need to tell you some things about Derek that would probably upset him. But these are things you need to know, especially now with all that's going on."

Nina gulped hard and took a forced breath.

"Okay, Don," she answered, not sure that it was.

Don told Nina Derek's real story, a past she'd never heard. He described a very troubled boy who had been abandoned, abused and endured a journey of racism, bullying and frequent fights. Don also shared several stories of Derek running away from home.

"I never knew that. I never knew of any of this," Nina said in disbelief. "Derek ran away?"

"Many times. One time, after a really bad beating he got from several boys, Derek disappeared for four days. It was during an especially hard winter with freezing rain and bone-chilling cold. We were worried sick and feared the worst. Then he just shows up. The police didn't know how he could have survived outside in those conditions."

"What happened?" Nina asked, dumbfounded.

"Well, everyone wanted to know that, including the police. He was beat to hell with a black eye, split lip and scrapes all over. The authorities suspected we might be abusing Derek and that's why he ran away."

"My God, Don."

"But after interviews with folks, including Derek, they dropped it and allowed him to stay with us."

"I don't understand Don. Where did he go? How did he survive that?"

"Well, that's the thing of it, Nina. We asked Derek that too." Don paused and took a deep breath. "He said he felt like someone was with him, watching over him." Don explained that Derek never ran away again after that. The boys that beat Derek so badly were scared from all the attention from police and teachers so they left Derek alone for awhile.

"Strange though ... years later, Derek didn't even seem to re-member the experience, which is probably why he never said any-thing to you about it," Don added.

"Derek never told me any of this. Why did the bullying go on for so long?" she finally asked.

Don cleared his throat but not his conscience. "At first I thought Derek should handle his problems himself, especially in his situation. I thought it would be good to let him stand on his own without his new dad stepping in," he said though that rationale sounded pathetic in his own ears. "I thought it would work itself out in time."

Don's voice grew thick. "Now I see how wrong I was. I didn't know just how bad it really was until years later." He stopped sud-denly and blew his nose. "I know Derek might be mad I'm telling you all this, but I stood on the sidelines when he had problems be-fore. I'll not do it again."

Over the next hour, Nina learned Derek's real history. Though Derek finished college in Colorado, he had started in Oklahoma. He was excited to wipe the slate clean and start over in college but it wasn't to be. A few of the same kids that were Derek's tormentors through the years ended up there as well, now as young men. They quickly spread stories, cruel vicious stories, about Derek across the campus. Derek left and ended up at the University of Colorado. This time, Derek's revision of his life worked and he left his past like a snake sheds its skin.

"Derek was a hard case with a hard head, Nina," Don chuckled, trying to lighten things. "We believe God challenges those he loves because it brings out their gifts. God had a whole lot of love for us," Don laughed though teary eyes. "The thing is, Nina, Derek's been on the run his whole life. He's been running from pain, his past, other people and especially himself. His life seemed to settle so much when he met you. But it sounds like his old ways are coming back to haunt him—and now you and the girls too."

Each word fell on Nina's heart like bombs and left her feeling empty and helpless. Her mind raced. *What was Derek running from now? Her?* She noticed he hardly even wore his wedding ring anymore and sometimes he didn't take it with him on his trips. *Where did this leave them as a family? Where could they go from here?*

Down the street at the park, Derek pushed Hannah in her swing as Bailey played tag with a few friends from the neighborhood. It was a gorgeous day but Derek felt like hell. Not only did he feel like a complete ass for what happened last night, but he was also nursing a terrible hangover. He had spent most of the morning dry heaving after vomiting violently into the toilet hours before. Derek knew Nina was as mad as she'd ever been since she didn't even bother to come downstairs to check on him as he retched.

Luckily, Hannah sang softly to herself and didn't demand Derek's attention. Derek watched her hair blowing back and forth as she kicked her little Mary Janes forward with each push. She lived her life from a genuine place but he was a fraud—a fake dad that merely made infrequent, disconnected appearances with his children.

He looked over at Bailey, busy with her friends, and felt miles away from her. Derek remembered when he was the center of her world and now he struggled to even be part of it. He used to carry her on his shoulders and she'd rub his ears, sweetly whispering, "Daddy, my loving Daddy." *God, she was so little then. Where did the time go?* A heavy weight of sadness descended and he had to look away.

Derek turned his aching head to thoughts of Nina and his past. He had only ever stuck with two things in his life, his job and Nina. He stuck with his job out of routine and fear. He had other dreams he was too frightened to pursue—or too lazy. Nina he'd stuck with out of pure love. She was a patch to his tattered spirit he'd never known before her. All he'd ever wanted to do was spend the rest of his life looking into her childlike eyes and holding her close. Now it seemed this too was in jeopardy and he knew it was his fault.

Everything he'd ever held dear seemed in peril. Was God, the merciless bully, now ripping his family away as he had Cole? He thought bitterly about the unanswered prayers as a child attending church with the Sorensens. Derek prayed that God would watch out for him, that the beatings and bullying would stop. He prayed his birth parents would find him and say they loved him. But God didn't care for him and never had.

Derek never told Nina about his past, and though he endured guilt for this omission, he believed lying to her about his past was the only way to keep her. Desperate to hold onto her, he didn't want to destroy her view of him by sharing his past. What if she left, wanting no part in someone even his birth parents didn't want, cast off by so many? Or someone who ran when times got hard? Or who had lied about himself? It seemed easier to let the past stay in the past.

"Daddy, can we go home now?" Hannah asked as she stared at the clouds. The words caught Derek by the heart. He desperately wanted to do just that but home, and all it meant, was crumbling around him as he stood there in the sun.

The next morning Derek packed in silence and Nina hustled after the children. They both busied themselves in their routines. Derek tried to catch Nina's eyes but she moved in and out of the room like a ghost.

Later that day the airplane touched down in Rapid City and Derek woke from a restless sleep. He recalled Arnold's question when they first met. Was he running *to* something or *away* from something? The words seemed to make sense now and formed a powerful question he needed to answer.

Once Derek registered at the hotel he tossed his bags onto the squeaking bed and stared at the giant purple stain on the carpet, wondering how he ended up here. He used to stay in five-star hotels, fly first class everywhere and have sales meetings catered by the finest restaurants. Now he stayed in pitiful roadside motels with blinking neon vacancy signs and beds that sagged like hammocks. He flew in puddle-jumping prop planes and had meetings in partly cleared storage rooms with snacks from the vending machine. Not wanting to keep falling deeper in despair, he changed his clothes, grabbed his shoes and headed for the road.

The first few minutes of the run, Derek battled the tightness in his lower back he'd often get from sitting in the cramped airplanes. Once that loosened he reveled in the picturesque fall afternoon in South Dakota. He saw rolling hills covered in golden prairie grass, rhythmically moving in the wind like waves. As he got deeper into the run, Derek quickened his pace and felt good.

Struck with a heightened sense of awareness, Derek scanned everything from the high puffy clouds down to the rocks and bottle caps on the roadside. Things never looked so vivid and sharp. He tasted the salt from sweat on his lips. He felt the wind rush over his skin and each beat of his heart. He smelled sweetgrass and road tar baking in the sun. He could hear the grasshoppers clicking and a faint hum of an approaching vehicle.

The exhausted delivery truck driver leaned over to grab the cigarette lighter that had fallen onto the floorboard of the passenger side. When he raised his eyes and lit his Marlboro, he drifted to the far side of the road where a man with dark hair was running directly ahead. He slammed on the brakes and locked his arms in panic. In a blink, he saw the man fly out away from the truck over the highway though he didn't hear the thud of an impact.

Like being hit by a bolt of lightning, Derek saw a bright burst of light and the feeling of electricity, but no pain. Was he being pulled or pushed? Derek lifted off the ground and could see the driver's terror through the windshield and blue smoke billowing out from the screeching tires. He had sailed through the air in peaceful silence, feeling lighter than air as he crossed the highway—and then everything went blank as he landed with a splash into a ditch filled with shallow stagnant water.

The driver jumped out of the truck, smelling the burnt rubber through a heavy cloud of dust and smoke. He'd chewed long black streaks into the pavement that continued into deep brown trails off the road into the soft grass. He ran as fast as his feet would carry him to the other side of the highway and felt sick when he got to the edge of the ditch. He saw the man lying face up in a bed of cattails and mud. The driver was sure he'd killed him and knew his life would never be the same. He stood there in shock and horror for a few moments, paralyzed, until he saw the man's eyes flutter and then open.

Derek opened his eyes and felt like he'd been taking a nap. He sat up and looked around. Covered in mud and cattail debris, he saw a disheveled and shaken man on the embankment above him. He slowly stood and climbed up the bank without any help from the terrified driver who stared blankly with his mouth wide open. The driver shyly asked if he was okay and Derek blankly nodded. He reviewed the incident in wonderment as he patted his body down, checking to make sure he had all his parts. He remembered now. But so did the driver, who now yelled at Derek, shifting from relief to anger.

"You crazy son of a bitch! I could have killed you! What the hell were you doing out here in the middle of nowhere?"

Derek's mind cleared and a quizzical grin appeared on his face, which enraged the driver further. He looked around at where he was and where he ended up, a distance of at least twenty-five feet. With squinting eyes and a mouth hanging open, finally realizing what just happened—what had been happening. He hadn't been hit by the truck. He surely hadn't jumped this far and he hadn't been dreaming. He had been flying!

Derek's mind still whirled with ideas the next day when he stopped at the town convenience store. He'd had a restless night, reviewing what happened and trying in vain to make any sense of it. Who would believe it? He still wasn't quite sure he believed it. The pressure of the secret pushed out from the inside. He desperately needed to share it but had no one to share it with.

He upgraded his breakfast from the watery coffee and stale bagel at the motel to a banana and a bottle of orange juice. As he walked down an aisle to the cashier, he saw a pair of familiar boots and braids behind a copy of *Field & Stream* magazine. "Hau Kola," Derek said, not knowing what the words actually meant but knew it was a greeting.

Arnold looked up and warmly smiled, "Hello to you too, friend."

The two stood outside the store in the shade of the overhang. He felt strangely connected to Arnold and couldn't figure out why. The man inspired calm and trust, but it was more than that. Maybe Arnold was a relative of his birth family. Actually Derek had entertained that idea with many Native people he met but this time he wanted to believe it. He also wanted to ask advice about what he'd experienced and guessed Arnold would be able to give it, but he didn't want to be judged a lunatic either.

"I've been thinking a lot about that question you asked when we first met. Am I running *away* from something or *to* something?"

Arnold sensed Derek's confusion then and now.

"You ever been to an inipi ceremony?" Arnold asked.

Nothing registered on Derek's face.

"You know, a sweatlodge ceremony?"

Derek shook his head.

"It's a purification ceremony we do to rid our mind, body and spirit of the junk we tend to gather on the journey. I'm having a group over to the house tonight for one. Would you like to go in with us?"

Derek didn't know anything about the ceremony, but the words "to rid our mind, body and spirit of the junk" resonated intensely and he jumped at this chance to attend.

In the past, Derek's attempts to fix his issues on his own only seemed to botch up his life further. It was like attempting brain surgery on himself, knowing there was malignant material but having no way to remove it. Derek desperately hoped the inipi ceremony would work for him. He confirmed the time with Arnold and headed off to the clinic.

Derek walked through the doors of the Indian Health Clinic and saw Sarah sitting in the lobby, focusing intently on her clipboard. He cleared his throat and Sarah quickly looked up, flashing a bright smile. "Oh hey, Derek. Good morning!"

"I've got the paperwork and stats on that x-ray machine you were interested in." They walked through the brightly lit hallways and could hear their shoes squeaking on the linoleum. They rounded a corner and went into a small meeting room to talk business. When the meeting was over, Sarah asked if Derek wanted to get a cup of coffee.

"So what do you think of our little community?" she asked as she unwrapped a granola bar.

Spirit on the Run 75

"I like it."

She smirked at him.

"Seriously, I do. It's quiet here and everyone I've met has been really nice."

The two talked about career and Sarah mentioned she'd visited San Diego several years ago. Derek relaxed.

"Sarah, can I ask your professional opinion on something?" She nodded as she sipped her coffee. "I have a friend who's been having these ... experiences." Derek cringed in his mind, hearing how lame this angle sounded but continued out of desperation. "He's had some experiences where he feels like he's flying. Or rather he thinks he *is* flying." Derek stopped there and held his breath.

"What, like in a dream?"

"No." Derek pulled his top lip in with his bottom teeth. "He's awake when it happens."

Sarah grinned.

"Yeah, I've seen that before," she said.

"You have?" Derek almost shouted his response.

She giggled and leaned forward. "It's called ... drugs!" Derek deflated and she saw it.

"No seriously, it could be anything, a cry for help, a mid-life crisis, a nervous breakdown, a schizophrenic hallucination—who knows?" She crunched a bite off of her granola bar. "Has your friend seen anyone about it, like a psychiatrist?"

Derek shook his head, looking worried.

"Or it could be ... he *needs* drugs," she said with a wink, as she stood to throw her cup and wrapper away.

Derek sat in his car, not sure if he should get out or not. Finally, after a few quick breaths, he opened the car door and walked up to the front of Arnold and Ruby's boxy, government-issued HUD pre-fab. Ruby answered the door of the small house with a big smile and reached out for his hand with both of hers, leading him inside.

"Toka hokshila, welcome to our home," Ruby said, beaming.

"Thank you." Derek glanced around at the humble house and felt out of place. Their home could only have been about a quarter of the size of his house and lacked the custom paint, oak floors, granite countertops and large screen TVs. Instead, it was cluttered with decorations, family pictures, and bundles of sweetgrass, Pendleton blankets, a lariat, a buffalo skull and Arnold's dusty boots by the back door. The floor creaked. In fact, it seemed the whole house shifted with each step. The air held heavy and delicious smells of cooking food. She led him the short distance to the back door, never letting go of his hands. "He's just there," she said, pointing with her lips to the backyard.

Derek followed a trail through a couple of rusted out cars, past an old refrigerator and then into a stand of cottonwood trees. He began to have doubts but continued. The path led to a small clearing with a bowl shaped depression. There sat a small dome-shaped lodge covered in what looked like olive drab Army tarps with an entry hole in the side. Arnold tended to a large fire not far from the lodge. Almost unrecognizable, Arnold had his hair unbraided and loose, and he wore gym shorts and a pair of shower sandals.

"Hau Kola," Arnold said through a thick cloud of white smoke.

"What does that mean, anyway?"

"It just means 'hi friend'," Arnold said as he poked the fire.

"Where's the rest of the group?"

Arnold looked up again, grinning. "This is the group, Kola."

Derek scanned around to confirm it.

"Like my moccasins?"

Derek looked at Arnold's foot rolling to and fro on the ground to display the shower sandals.

"They're Adidas."

"What's all this?" Derek asked as he pointed at a pile of rocks in the fire.

"We're heating these grandfathers up to take into the sweat with us. They're going to guide us, to listen to us in there." Derek looked around for the group of old men that Arnold mentioned.

"The rocks, Derek," Arnold pointed with his lips. Derek looked at the pile of rocks in the center of the bonfire and then to the dark opening that lead into the lodge.

"Are we going in there?" Derek asked, already knowing the answer.

"Yep."

Derek asked questions about the ceremony and what they'd be doing. Arnold patiently answered every question, explaining the protocols, the reasons and the flow of the ceremony. Derek sighed in relief, knowing his only responsibility would be to pray and bring the rocks into the lodge. Arnold would do everything else.

Derek felt obligated to offer something, so he dug in his wallet and opened it up. "I wanted to thank you for doing all this, Arnold." Derek handed several twenties forward and was stopped by a wave of Arnold's hand.

"No, Kola."

"But I wanted to give this …"

"We don't do that around here," Arnold said, firmly rejecting the offer. "I serve where I'm called."

"But I didn't call you," Derek said as he stuffed the money back into his wallet.

"Sure you did," Arnold said smiling. "Remember when you asked me for directions in front of the store when we first met?"

Derek nodded.

Arnold waved his hand toward the fire and the lodge. "Well, I'm offering this one to you."

The two stood around the fire and talked. Derek found that Arnold had quite a storied life. He was a former bronc rider and traveled the country in rodeos for many years. "Is that where you got all those scars?" Derek asked looking at the dime-sized scars covering Arnold's chest.

"No, these are from Sun Dance ceremony."

"What about that one?" Derek asked, looking at the long furrow running down Arnold's left cheek from his eye.

"No, horses don't stab you. I got that in prison."

Derek's mouth hung open.

"I served time for borrowing a car when I was younger."

"They sent you to prison for *that*?"

"Well, yeah, when you do it five times," Arnold said in amusement. "I was a knucklehead back then. I wasn't pressured or influenced; I had only myself to blame. I could never live up to the tough guy image I held in my own mind." Arnold looked up at Derek. "Hell, I'd been a bronc rider since age ten, fought all the time and look at my name, Kills Straight." Arnold slapped his chest. "I *had* to be some kind of bad ass Indian." He looked into the fire, laughing to himself.

"I've heard what doesn't kill us makes us stronger," Derek said, trying to offer solace that wasn't needed.

"I don't know about that. But I do know that what doesn't kill us can make us smarter," Arnold said with a wink and Derek nodded in agreement.

Arnold explained what they were to do next to get ready for the sweat and stoked the fire one last time.

"It's time, Derek."

Derek felt embarrassed as he got undressed in broad daylight. He felt fatter and looked fatter than he remembered. He stripped down to just his shorts and Arnold pointed his chin at Derek's watch.

"That too."

Derek removed his watch.

"Well, I know you don't know what tribe you are Derek, but I think you're at least part white," Arnold said pointing to Derek's wrist. Where the watch had been, it looked like a patch of cream spilled on a redwood table. They both laughed.

Arnold first loaded his carved, slender pipe with tobacco, offering prayers in the Lakota language as he did. Derek tried his best to look reverent and follow Arnold's directions. "The lodge is built small and low like this so we have to enter by crawling on hands and knees. It keeps us humble." Arnold crawled in and sat near the entrance with a set of deer antlers and a hand drum. "Okay, now start bringing those grandfathers in here."

Derek made trip after trip to the fire pit to clumsily balance a red hot rock on the tines of the pitchfork. When he brought each one in, Arnold would use the deer antlers as a tool to push and maneuver each rock into a small hole carved in the earth in the center of the lodge. As he went back and forth, Derek pondered the ceremony and what it would be like. He was nervous and now he was glad it was just him and Arnold.

After all twenty-eight rocks were retrieved, Arnold asked Derek to bring the tin bucket of water to the door. There was a hollow buffalo horn floating in it.

"Now come on in," Arnold said quietly.

Derek crawled into the darkened lodge. It smelled like wet dirt and sage. Arnold pulled out small pinches of bright green foliage out of a leather pouch and put them on the rocks.

"It's cedar," he said. "Good medicine." The little pieces of cedar sizzled and popped, releasing a pungent, sweet smell as it smoked. Derek felt good in here. He felt safe. Arnold pulled the bucket into the lodge and shut the flap that served as the door. All the light was gone except for a faint red light in the rocks and the dying embers of the cedar.

Arnold began playing the hand drum and singing in his language. Derek remembered Arnold explaining earlier that he would sing to invite the spirits into the lodge and to ask that the Creator would hear their prayers. Derek let his mind wander to images of his family and prayed. Maybe God would listen to him in here since he didn't seem to listen in church. Derek couldn't see a thing now but he heard a gurgle of water as the buffalo horn was filled from the bucket. A loud hiss followed each time Arnold poured the water onto the rocks. Derek was assaulted with wave after wave of hot steam as Arnold sang louder and stronger. Derek didn't understand the words being sung, but he could feel the emotion behind it. Arnold seemed to be appealing to the spirits, almost begging, for something.

Images from Derek's life paraded randomly through his head like a slideshow. He saw his girls, himself as a boy, Nina's smiling face and the Sorensens. He saw his co-workers, his tormentors from childhood and Kay. He could see Arnold in his mind and Ruby next to him. Then he saw Cole. He imagined holding the tiny baby in his arms.

Suddenly the singing seemed far away. The severe heat faded and Derek had that electric current pulsing through him again. In his mind, Derek saw intense, vibrant colors flashing but no clear images. A channel, a portal, to someplace else was opening up for him. Something softly brushed past him, moving the air over his skin and leaving goose bumps in its wake. The music stopped, and the lodge grew quiet except for an unintelligible whisper as new images began to appear.

Derek stood in the doorway to the bathroom watching Nina pour breast milk down the drain as she sobbed. This loving nourishment had been meant for Cole, coming from Nina's own body, from her very heart. But now it went down the drain, unfulfilled in its purpose. Wasted. Derek watched this gut-wrenching scene because he couldn't look away. Nina looked up with puffy, red eyes as if expecting Derek to stop her, wanting him to stop her.

Next, Derek stood at Cole's graveside, holding a carved angel with wire wings. The angel held a baby in her arms. Love eternal. The memorial was over and Derek stood there long after everyone left. Nina asked if he wanted her and the girls to stay but he didn't. He could feel the machinery of his life slowing down and the fires going out.

In that moment Derek started running though his legs never moved. In his mind, he ran to get away from everything and everyone, consciously disconnecting, to lick these wounds that had ripped him open. He had been reminded again just how temporary the elements of his life were and how pain would be there waiting for him as it always had been.

The memorial service now floated by in a blur of saddened handshakes and hugs, gloomy faces and words that fell short of any aid. Derek couldn't wait for it to be over, but it lasted much of the day. He didn't want to mingle or eat and he didn't want to tell people he was okay, this all was okay, because it wasn't. Instead, he made frequent and long trips to the bathroom where he'd pull out Cole's blue knitted cap and stare at it. He had no tears, no words. Derek recalled the moment he'd gently pulled it off Cole's head.

The nurses were soberly shutting down the equipment and disconnecting the tubes and tape that were meant to be lifelines but looked more like shackles. It was the first time he and Nina saw Cole's face unobstructed by medical tape. He was so beautiful, so perfect. He seemed as if he was peacefully sleeping. It was bitter-sweet temptation to believe that lie, even for a moment. But Cole was gone and all Derek had was this tiny blue cap in his helpless hands.

In the next image, Derek looked down at his own feet as he ran along a road. He saw his feet leaving the ground and for a moment, he was afraid. The fear quickly passed, feeling like he was in a dream and safe from real danger. He ran faster and faster and could feel the electric current build in its intensity. It pulsed and exploded through his system. He felt euphoria, love, exhilaration and joy. He felt full of life itself.

Derek steadily rose off the pavement higher and higher. He heard a whisper he couldn't understand as he passed over trees, through a flock of birds and into the clouds. Derek was now frozen amongst stars and looking around. He could see the earth, other planets in the distance. When he turned to find the sun, Derek saw Arnold's face instead, illuminated by the now opened doorway to the lodge.

"We're done, Derek. Washte inipi," Arnold said, rousing Derek from the reverie. "Good sweat."

Derek cleared his head and crawled clockwise around the pit of warm rocks on his hands and knees to leave the lodge. As he stood up, he was grateful his tears were hidden by the sweat that covered him from head to toe. He was still dazed from what he'd just experienced.

Arnold retrieved his pipe from a mound of dirt next to the lodge and lit the bowl. He puffed on the pipe, and as he blew out the smoke, he again offered prayers. He looked content, almost happy. Arnold handed the pipe to Derek who did the same.

As the two men dressed quietly, Derek felt drained. He'd had high expectations for this ceremony, hoping it would fix him and resolve his problems. The experience was intense beyond measure but what the hell did it all mean? Wasn't he supposed to be better now? He felt empty.

"I don't feel healed," Derek finally blurted in frustration. "Wasn't this supposed to help me get rid of the junk I've gathered on my journey?" Derek asked, using Arnold's words. Arnold merely grinned, as a professor would to a new student, as he put on a pair of sweat pants.

"It's not supposed to *heal* you, Kola. It's to show you ways to heal yourself."

Derek's mind swirled in confusion.

"Whatever happened in there was meant for you to fulfill that purpose," Arnold explained.

Derek was puzzled. Which part of this whole experience was meant to heal him, the images of flying or the awful memories? And what was all that whispering during the ceremony? Was that Arnold mumbling or Derek's own confused thoughts? Or was it something else?

"Come on. Ruby's got some food ready." The two men walked back to the house and were greeted by the smells of venison with onion gravy, carrots, potatoes and frybread. They were also each given an ice tea and a big hug from Ruby. The trio had a nice conversation but Derek's mind couldn't leave the sweatlodge and what had happened to him there. He kept reviewing the visions, wondering which one was the key. He felt like a kid digging his fingers into change slots on vending machines, looking for treasures but coming up short.

"So tell us about your family, Derek," Ruby said as she forked a piece of meat. Pangs of guilt and regret hit Derek as he explained how truly ideal his family was. As wonderful as they were, he had been the weak link in the chain when he should have been their anchor. He thought of his past, his dishonesty with Nina.

"How did you two meet?" Derek asked, shifting the subject.

He admired the strong connection these two had and was curious how it began. With a glow in her eyes, Ruby told the story of a young man with long legs and a tall Stetson at the tribal rodeo tournament. He was cocky and turned her off at first, but he was a man to behold on the back of that bronco.

"It was like he was dancing with death on the back of that thing," Ruby said with wide eyes.

Arnold grinned as he ate.

"In time, I found out what kind of man he really was," Ruby said.

Derek saw a chance to justify his own lies. "It must have been hard to accept his past, I mean with jail time and all?"

"No, not really. He told me the truth and that's all I ever wanted. I saw the man and not his past record," she said and playfully poked Arnold's ribs. "And lucky for him it's stayed that way."

Derek cowered inside, ashamed.

Later that evening Derek lay in his squeaky bed of sandpaper sheets staring at the popcorn ceiling. He couldn't get the beautiful images from the sweat out of his head but what he really needed was answers. He felt ripped off, let down by a ceremony that didn't deliver closure. He kicked the linens off his legs and sighed, feeling he was running out of options. Maybe he did need counseling—or drugs.

Derek sat up in bed and decided to go for a run. He wasn't able to sleep and maybe the fresh air would help him think. After he donned his clothes and shoes he exited the motel and heard the buzz of the neon sign by the road. Derek stretched for a few minutes and trotted across the gravel parking lot. As he neared the sign he heard a sizzling pop and then several letters suddenly went dark.

What timing, he thought and continued running.

Derek ran along the roadside, looking up at the diamond-like stars but trying to be wary of the occasional car. A truck drove by and Derek barely noticed one headlight flickered wildly like a strobe and then abruptly went dark. The moment was lost on him as he grew more focused on his run.

Frustration bubbled up inside of him, like the sweat now accumulating on the surface of his skin. As Derek ran faster he revisited Arnold's question. *Was he running to something or away from something?* As he ran ever faster in the quiet of the night, he heard a voice.

Clearly and softly the voice asked, "Why are you so angry?"

CHAPTER 6

DEREK ABRUPTLY STOPPED in his tracks. He was
sure he'd just heard a child's voice. Now all he could hear was his
heavy breathing and his pounding heart. He looked around, but
inky darkness hid everything. He heard a frog croak. A sudden
breeze crawled up his neck and rattled the leaves of the cottonwoods. Fear filled Derek. Like a child alone in a haunted house, he
bolted in panic.

Running as fast as his feet would carry him, he looked backward as he crossed the motel's dirt parking lot. He slammed into a
40-gallon drum that served as the garbage can and went over the
top, landing in a pile of fast food wrappers and aluminum cans.
Oblivious to the mess or the impact, he quickly scrambled to his
feet in a cloud of dust and hobbled backward to his room. The
motel owner came out to investigate the commotion just as Derek
shut the door.

Derek's shaking hands turned his room key to lock the door
and then fumbled with the safety chain. In the lamplight of his
room, he collapsed into a chair and closed his eyes. He rocked back
and forth and desperately chanted, "That wasn't a voice. It was
nothing." It took all his willpower to finally pull back the curtain a
bit to make sure all was clear outside.

After little sleep, the morning came as an unwelcome sight to Derek. He had to button his shirt three times to get it right. He thought about the voice he heard so clearly last night, wondering if it was real or imagined.

He wandered out to the lobby and saw Sarah perusing a copy of *People* magazine. She looked up and smiled.

The two walked out to her car and got into it.

Sarah noticed how rattled Derek looked in the passenger seat of her car and finally asked, "Are you alright?"

Derek didn't try to dodge the question. He was in crisis. He told Sarah about the incident, fully expecting her to recommend immediate counseling or medical attention. Maybe he needed it. Instead she seemed suspiciously collected to Derek when he mentioned he'd heard a disembodied voice. Her momentary silence tormented him as the mile markers passed.

"What do you think?" Derek finally blurted.

"I think you should talk back."

This was the last thing Derek expected Sarah to say.

"Look, there are two ways to look at this. If you want my medical opinion, I could say seek help, you may need counseling, meds, you may be a schizophrenic or experiencing a breakdown. But in our Native culture, we have a different view of these things."

Derek looked at her expectantly but Sarah focused on the road ahead. He was suspended in the moment.

"And …?" Derek impatiently asked.

"I think you should talk back."

"Hello?" Nina asked, cradling the phone on her shoulder as she struggled to brush Hannah's hair despite whines and wiggles.

"Hi Nina. This is Don. I just wanted to check in and see how you were holding up."

Nina mumbled through a barrette clenched between her teeth. "Oh, I'm okay. Derek's on the road or I'd let you talk with him."

"No, that's alright darlin'. I called to talk with you."

Don and Nina talked for the better part of an hour, a bit about the kids, a bit about the weather, but mostly about Derek. Nina had time to think since their last phone call and asked questions about Derek's youth. It seemed strange to get information about her husband of ten years from another person, even if it was her father-in-law. Realizing how little she knew about many parts of Derek's life made her feel even more detached from him.

The story that was most revealing to Nina was about Derek's prom. Nina was under the impression that Derek hadn't attended his prom. At least, that's what he'd told her.

"I think that whole thing tore him up pretty bad," Don said.

Don told Nina of Derek's crush on the co-captain of the cheerleading squad. Despite Derek's troubles and usual brooding, Kelly had often shown him kindness and that was precious to Derek. Don went on to say that Rory McCloud knew of Derek's crush and saw it as an exploitable weakness where he could deal a blow far more hurtful than any punch to the face. Rory's warfare against Derek had gotten more exacting and more sophisticated as they grew older. Rory and his friends pressured Kelly to do something unconscionable in asking Derek to the prom as a practical joke.

"Derek was overjoyed," Don said with a quivering voice. "He hadn't planned on going to the prom, so all the tuxes in town were rented. He ended up wearing an old pale green suit of mine, dated for sure and a bit threadbare in parts, but it was the only one that fit him. Derek wore it like it was a royal cloak. He smiled wider than we'd seen since the day we asked him to come live with us. He ironed his own shirt, polished his church shoes to a gloss. Derek wanted everything to be perfect."

Don told Nina they let Derek borrow their only car—a 1967 Pontiac LeMans.

"She was old, but she was classy," Don said with pride. "Derek spent all day washing and waxing it. I can still see him driving out of the parking lot with his pine green bow tie, the flowers he'd picked and arranged. And that smile." Don got choked up remembering the moment. "We were so proud of him. It seemed things were getting better for Derek and he was finally being accepted, but then it all went sideways."

Nina hadn't noticed she'd been holding her breath. "What happened, Don?"

"We got a call not an hour after he left. He'd lost control of the car and ended up half wrapped around a tree outside of town."

"My God," Nina gasped.

"We showed up at the hospital and thank the Lord he was okay. He got banged up pretty good. The car was totaled."

Don went on to explain that Derek had showed up to Kelly's house to pick her up and saw her standing on her front porch with Todd McCormick, captain of the football team, and her date for the prom all along. A group of more than thirty kids, including Rory McCloud, stood on Kelly's front lawn. They all pointed and jeered at Derek as he pulled up. When he stepped out of the car to try and talk to Kelly, the group pelted Derek and the car with eggs and hysterical laughter. Derek's suit, pressed shirt, the car and even his shoes were covered in runny egg and shattered shells.

In a full blown rage, Derek slammed the door and the gas pedal. He squealed out of the neighborhood in shame to the delight of the crowd and to tears streaming down Kelly's face for the terrible role she'd agreed to play. Derek sped out of town, headed anywhere but prom or home. In a turn, he lost control of the car and slammed into an oak tree off the side of the highway.

"How horrible," Nina said quietly.

"We felt so bad for Derek, but helpless at the same time. I was angry about the car, too, which probably didn't help things. There were many tense weeks in our house following that mess."

Nina frowned. Of course she felt pity after hearing such a sad tale, but with each layer of his concealed past life peeled back, Derek seemed more and more a stranger to her.

Skip put the finishing touches on his latest sales report when Sedgewick appeared in the doorway like a specter. He held a folder in his hand and looked like someone who'd just run over the neighbor's cat.

"What's going on, boss?"

"I just got done talking with HR and ..." Sedgewick halted. "Have you heard from Derek today?"

"No, not today," Skip answered.

He quickly realized what was going on after sizing up the personnel folder, the visit to HR and now Sedgewick's query. Derek was about to be kicked while he was down and get the axe from Global Medix. Skip had been outraged with Derek for the blow out and false accusation, but this was his friend. Skip flipped mental switches and became the quintessential salesman that earned him his stripes in the company.

"I do know he's been working his tail off in some pretty tough locations," Skip said with firmness. "And in most places, since they're *so rural*," Skip emphasized, "he hasn't had cell phone coverage."

"Well, he should be checking in more," Sedgewick grumbled to his watch. Skip could see the guilt monkeys were climbing onto Sedgewick's back.

"Mr. Sedgewick," Skip added dramatic pause. "Derek knows he dropped the ball, but he's eager to prove he belongs on the varsity. He's on injured reserve right now but he's working hard to heal. You'll see. He'll be scoring touchdowns again soon."

Skip wanted to give himself a high five as he saw Sedgewick's game face start to appear.

"Well, alright then. Tell him to check in more," Sedgewick said before turning on his heel and disappearing.

Back in South Dakota, Derek sat alone at a local diner in a booth made for six. The deep cushion and vinyl cover of the bench seat made a variety of embarrassing noises each time he shifted weight, sounding much like Bailey's fart machine keychain she got last year for her birthday. Each time he moved, the sound produced made the wait staff and the other patrons glare.

He looked over at an old man with his pewter hair shining with Bryl Cream as he sadly nursed a cup of coffee. How pathetic the old guy looked, sitting in his big booth alone, then Derek realized he was in the same pathetic boat.

Derek wiped the spaghetti sauce from his mouth before he fumbled to get his cell phone. The burgundy bench seat let one rip. Derek saw the number and decided to answer it. The last several weeks had been a torture of guilt and shame since his drunken blow out with Nina and Skip.

"Hi Nina," Derek said.

"I wanted to call and check on you. Were you ever going to call?"

"Well, yeah. I've just been busy."

Nina let the lie go.

"How is everybody doing?" Derek asked.

"We're good. The girls have been keeping me on the run as usual." To Nina, the conversation resembled the clumsy kind you have when dating someone new, someone you didn't know very well.

"I talked to Pappa Don earlier today," she offered.

"That's good. How are they?"

"They're doing fine, but we talked about you mostly."

Derek immediately felt suspicious and outnumbered as he asked, "About what exactly?"

Nina came clean with the conversation she'd had. Derek sat listening and could feel his pulse beating in his ears. He'd lost his appetite and set down his fork. What incensed him even more was that he could hear the threads of sympathy start to weave their way into Nina's voice as she repeated the painful stories of his past life. The sharp pieces of his childhood he'd tried so hard to conceal were now under a spotlight. When she got to the story of prom night, the horrible memories touched off explosions in Derek's head. He'd had enough of this ambush.

"Stop it!" Derek barked.

The old man looked up from his coffee.

"How dare you stroll down memory lane about private parts of my life!"

"Private?" Nina fired back. "We're supposed to be honest with each other, not keep secrets. It makes me worry about what else you're not telling me. We're drowning in this darkness, Derek!"

"Well, then let's be open about it," Derek said sarcastically, lowering his voice as he paid the bill and stood to leave. "I guess you know why Mom has a limp then, right?"

"Of course. She had a car accident years ago."

The line was quiet.

"Right, Derek? She was in a car accident."

"Oh, you've got to hear this one if we're ripping my life open tonight. After the accident on prom night, the car was totaled. My mom worked at a day care center in town and depended on that car to get back and forth to work."

Derek told Nina that Martha had elected to walk to work and back, telling Don that getting fresh air and exercise walking alongside the road would do her good. One rainy morning, a car on the road hit Martha. She'd shattered her hip in the accident, and even after several surgeries, the leg was never the same.

"I did that, Nina. Me!" Derek's voice wavered and sounded more desperate than angry. "Every time I look at my mom and her painful limp, I carry the shame of what I did to cause it."

The silence cut both ways now.

"Are you happy now? Now you know what a great guy you married."

"Derek, you can't put that on yourself. It was an accident."

"Easy for you to say. You don't carry a burden like that." Derek hissed. "You can't possibly imagine what it's like to look at someone you love and wonder if secretly they blame you for their pain."

"Can't I, Derek? I've felt ever since …"

"If there are no other wounds you'd like to reopen tonight, and no other surprises for me, then I have to go."

"I had no idea you could be so cruel," Nina said. "And that's a surprise to me."

The sound of a click announced the call was over and Nina felt more alone than ever.

Hannah kept pushing her long, unkempt hair out of her eyes. She busily drew a picture at the breakfast bar with crayons spread across the table. The crayons kept rolling to Bailey's side of the table as she tried to finish her math homework.

"Keep the crayons on your side," Bailey snapped.

Hannah kept drawing as if she hadn't heard, swinging her legs in the chair.

"What are you drawing anyway?" Bailey asked.

"A picture of what my room will look like in heaven."

"What? Let me guess—everything pink and a big TV with SpongeBob always on?" Bailey peeked over at the picture.

"This is my bed and this is Cole's crib. See? There's Cole." Hannah beamed. Most everything was indeed pink.

"You better not let Mom see that," Bailey said, adjusting her glasses and twisting the end of her long braid. "She might get upset."

Hannah continued, intently working on her drawing.

"Are Mommy and Daddy getting a force?"

"A what?" Bailey asked, even more annoyed than before.

"A force. You know, when they don't live together anymore."

"It's a *divorce*, dummy. And no, they're not."

Hannah looked relieved at the answer.

Bailey wanted to believe her own words, but so far this year it had happened to two kids in her class. Divorce seemed to be going around like the flu. The simple fact was Bailey couldn't imagine her parents getting divorced, so she chose not to entertain the thought and wouldn't let Hannah think about it either. Just like the troll that she used to think lived under her bed, once she stopped believing in it, then it couldn't exist or hurt her. She was hopeful this was the same type of thing.

Nina and Kay sat in the living room, drinking green tea and eating Oreos.

"We don't talk anymore and when we do, it's an argument," Nina told her mother. "I wish it was like it used to be." Nina stopped herself. She had been living under a veil about Derek's past and didn't want to go back to being ignorant. "Or maybe I wish we were more like you and Dad were."

"Oh don't just go painting beautiful rainbows and forget the storms." Kay picked up an Oreo, using it to point at Nina. "Your dad and I fought over many things."

Nina seemed incredulous.

"Over what?" Nina had only wonderful, beautiful memories of her parents and saw her soft-spoken father as beyond reproach.

"His family for one."

Nina's disbelief showed clearly. Her late grandparents had always seemed warm, even if somewhat formal to her mother.

"Your grandparents didn't care much for me or their son's decision to marry a foreigner. Plus we argued about cultural differences, money, all kinds of things. We came from two different worlds and had a lot of challenges," Kay explained.

"I never knew," Nina seemed dazed at how many new things she was learning about those around her.

"Well, you wouldn't have. We never argued in front of you," Kay said and popped the Oreo into her mouth.

"We didn't used to either, but that practice has gone out the window." Nina furrowed her brow and looked away. She reached down and softly cradled her tea in both hands. "I feel so bad for the girls and try to shield them from it as best as I can."

Nina admitted to her mom that the last year had been an endless series of battles that had left open wounds that didn't have time to heal before the next clash. Nina even admitted that she sometimes said things to get a reaction from Derek just so he would talk to her.

"I miss him so much, Mom. It feels like being on an ocean and dying of thirst. You want the … no, you *need* the refreshment of the water so bad that out of desperation, you go for the salt water—even if it ends up doing you in." Nina moaned at her own observation. "How pathetic is that?" Nina tried to laugh through the pain.

Kay took a sip of her tea.

"How could it have gotten this bad?" Nina asked, staring into her cup of tea for the answers. "So much of Derek's life has been kept from me. It's caused doubt for both of us." Nina sighed. "I just don't know how to bridge the gaps anymore."

"You're not thinking of divorce are you?"

"No Mom, no way," Nina said, shaking her head. "We'll work it out somehow."

"I know you will, my *sakura*," Kay said as she took Nina's hand and gently patted it.

Nina had been doing all she knew how to do to keep the family intact. She felt more each day that she was married to a man she didn't know anymore, maybe never did. Talking with her mom, Nina realized that if this mess was going to change for the better, it had to be Derek's decision. Nina hoped Derek would come around before too much damage was done to their relationship and the girls. All she could do was continue trying. Nina loved Derek too much to give up on them—at least she desperately hoped she did.

Derek was sure he'd made the waitress angry. He'd showed up to eat breakfast at a truck stop diner that served the greasy spoon fare, but wanted something different. He ordered instant oatmeal and wondered why it tasted slightly like coffee. He looked over the counter and saw the head cook angrily mumbling as he dumped the rest of the water out of the glass coffee pot he'd used to heat it. Derek also ordered yogurt. The waitress spent ten minutes searching in the back before gruffly planting the cup of yogurt on the table in front of him. Derek waited until she walked away to read the expiration date and found it was three days overdue.

As he left the diner and got into his Hyundai Accent rental car, his phone vibrated. Without looking at the caller ID, he picked it up. "Hello?"

"Hi Derek. It's Skip." Skip sounded detached.

"Hey Skip." Derek was at a loss. "How's things?"

"Listen. You need to call and check in with Sedgewick more often. He's having a tizzy on our end, thinking you've gone Native on us. Ah, those were his words … no offense."

Derek was happy to hear his friend's voice.

"Yeah, that sounds like Sedgewick alright," he said.

"I just wanted you to know so ..." Skip trailed off. "Anyway, you don't want to get into more trouble. So, just thought you should know."

"Thanks, Skip," Derek said. "Thanks a lot."

Derek couldn't bring himself to apologize to Skip for his drunken blowout but made a commitment that he would. He was still too embarrassed to bring it up.

"No problem. That's what friends are for, right? Gotta go."

Derek was grateful he didn't have a chance to say anything else before Skip got off the line.

All the signs pointed to a run. The weather was perfect. The sun hung between its apex and the horizon. A slight breeze filled with fragrances of sage and pine gently blew across the plains. But Derek stood motionless on the side of the road and worried about hearing the voice again. It took every effort just to put his running clothes on and lace up his shoes. One moment he would decide to head back to his room and watch TV. The next moment he'd come back to his spot on the side of the road. After fifteen minutes of wavering, Derek figured he was being ridiculous. Besides, the light of day made the incident in the dark from days earlier seem like pure fantasy.

Derek cautiously trotted down the edge of the road. His eyes darted around. He watched for traffic and the source of the voice he'd heard so clearly. Derek's trot became a jog. Sweat began to appear around his neck and his muscles loosened. He listened to the rhythmic thrum of his shoes hitting the gravel and began to relax. A red-tailed hawk spun on one wing and then the other, dancing in the air with no apparent purpose but to dance.

The sweat came freely now and he started thinking about Arnold and the inipi ceremony. Though still confused about what answers he was meant to get from the ceremony, he felt reconnected afterward and wanted to do it again. Though he had never done an inipi before, it seemed familiar to him. Derek recalled the darkness, the hot rocks and the hiss of the steam as he accelerated.

A small tingle grew from his chest and down his arms to his fingers. He picked up his pace, enjoying the sensation. The electric pulsing flowed down his legs into his feet. He ran faster. He thought of the missing footprints at the beach, the near miss with the truck. He ran faster. He thought of Nina, Bailey and Hannah. He thought of holding Cole in his arms.

A familiar buzz and gentle pressure reached a crescendo and enveloped Derek like a body suit of static electricity. Suddenly he noticed the sound of his feet hitting the roadside was gone. He couldn't hear the wind or the rustle of prairie grass. Derek looked down and saw he was still running, but several inches off the road. As he tried in vain to process what was happening, the gentle voice returned.

"Can you hear me?"

"Y-y-yes," Derek answered, wide-eyed and frazzled.

"Where are we?"

"South Dakota," Derek said but wondered if that was really the answer to the question.

"Where's Hannah?"

"At home," Derek said.

"Home …" the voice repeated back quietly.

Derek glanced down and dared not quit running now. He was now a foot or two off the ground! He had broken through the once sturdy membrane that used to separate sanity and lunacy.

Like most people, Derek had experienced a running internal dialogue in his mind since his earliest memories, a muted conversation that came as thoughts he already knew. What made this voice so disturbing is that it had something previously missing—it had *volume.* Plus the voice had a distinct speech pattern and sound very different from his, which made it truly puzzling.

Derek decided he would surely admit himself to a clinic and demand meds as soon as he returned home, but for now he would play along with this insane scenario. Maybe Sarah was right. After all, he was having hallucinations of floating and talking with a voice inside his head. It all seemed surreal and yet strangely pleasant. He continued to run as the sweat beaded freely over his head and neck. This completely redefined Derek's idea of a runner's high.

"Am I going crazy?" he asked the voice.

"No."

Derek smirked at the answer, thinking it was like the fox guarding the henhouse.

"Why are you here now, talking to me?"

"I don't know," the voice admitted after a long pause. "I'm not sure."

Derek imagined how the folks back home would react to this scene. Or a passerby. Reality was melting away and Derek embraced it. He decided to play a game with the voice inside his head.

"What did I have for breakfast this morning?"

"Nothing," the voice answered. "But you should have eaten something."

"What color is my rental car?" Derek's pace slowed and the voice came back quiet and garbled so he sped up and asked the question again.

"Metallic sage green."

Derek thought the answer odd. He was thinking green so why did the voice answer so specifically? Was this his conscience or something else?

"Why are you so angry?" the voice asked Derek.

Derek now wondered whether this was his conscience or his therapist. He worked hard to keep his pace up and saw he still ran several feet above the ground. Instead of answering, he asked another question.

"What did I always want to be when I grew up?"

"A superhero."

Derek delighted in the answer, but knew it was too easy.

"You still do," the voice added.

Derek could feel the intense, warm energy surrounding him, lifting him up. If he was hallucinating, his fantasy of flight should have lifted him higher off the ground than a couple feet. He stretched out his hands to the side, adding to his flying experience. Going crazy felt wonderful.

Derek had read somewhere that our subconscious holds all the material we've ever learned, even some we don't realize we learned. The only challenge to this phenomenon was accessing the information. But since his subconscious seemed so willing to talk, he'd see what he knew.

"What was the combination to my high school locker?"

Derek was certain he hadn't remembered this one. He'd even forgotten it while he was actually in high school.

"9-21-3," the voice said without hesitation.

Amazing!

Derek reviewed all the other strange happenings and began to doubt this was something strictly in his own mind. Derek struggled to keep his pace. He worried the voice would leave him again when he stopped running, so he focused and asked the question he wasn't sure he wanted the answer to.

"Is it you doing this, the floating thing?" Derek was gasping for precious air. "Was it you on the beach that day and in front of the truck?"

"Yes."

Derek felt a tickle at the back of his neck.

"Is it you burning the lights out?"

"I think so," the voice sounded a bit ashamed.

"Why do you only show up when I run?"

"I don't know."

"Are you going to stay with me?" Derek wasn't sure what he wanted to hear.

The childlike voice seemed to be considering the question in the silence that followed. "I'm not sure."

Frustrated, Derek struggled and panted like an animal, using all his strength to keep his legs moving. Talking to this voice reminded him of the liquid-filled eight balls in childhood that would float up a plastic pyramid to the clear window that seemed to answer any question posed to it. The answers seemed random, mysterious, and yet seemed to always fit.

Maybe this is what Harvey at the shoe store was talking about, a runner's high to the extreme. A near spiritual experience of talking directly to one's subconscious. Knowing he couldn't continue much longer, he asked the question that seemed to matter more than any other.

"Is this my subconscious?" Derek asked, unsure if he could handle the answer, and slowed his pace.

The voice came back garbled and too low to hear.

Derek's connection to the voice seemed to be like tuning a radio. Derek had to quicken his pace to dial it back in but only caught the tail end of the transmission.

"... I've come to you."

Derek thought he might vomit from exertion. He began to panic, thinking of what this all meant. Runner's high or not, hearing voices in one's head was not a good thing.

"Why am I hearing a voice in my head? Why is this happening to me?" Derek had a feeling he wouldn't hear the answer and couldn't run anymore anyway. He was about to slow his pace when the answer came like a whirlwind.

"... Because I love you, Daddy."

CHAPTER 7

DEREK SAT SILENTLY in his motel room, looking at his palms, which were oozing blood from deep trenches. Gravel had viciously chewed his hands and filled the cuts with splinters and road tar. He'd washed them as well as he could but they still looked a mess. After hearing those haunting words, he had stopped running and crashed violently onto the roadside. How could he keep running after hearing that?

Derek's packed suitcase was beside him but he couldn't rise from his seat on the edge of the bed. His knees ached terribly and too many questions swirled through his head to allow him to move. His cell phone beeped and his unblinking eyes finally fluttered. It was a message from the airlines reminding him to be on his way if he wanted to make it home tonight.

Like a zombie, he stood, grabbed his bag and walked slowly to the car. He turned the ignition but couldn't put the car in gear. He closed his eyes and a flood of memories burst forth inside of him, crumbling the walls that had held them in place for so long— seeing his baby son again and remembering the hurt, the guilt, the fear, the shame, the anger. *Was the voice really him?*

With a crumbling voice, Derek choked out the words, "Oh my Cole ... my little boy." Tears rimmed his eyes.

The gravity of the moment pulled Derek deeper into his seat. He managed a shaky whisper, "Is it really you, Cole?" He placed his hands to his face and broke down in convulsed, uncontrolled sobs that poured stinging tears into his wounded hands.

That night Arnold Kills Straight looked up at the sky. The steam from his coffee looked like a ghost version of a fire as it hit the cool air.

"Are you coming in?" Ruby asked with a gray and purple Pendleton wrapped tightly around her shoulders. "It's getting late."

Arnold turned and smiled warmly at his wife.

"Go ahead and hit the sack. I'm going to stay up. There's something going on with our kola."

Ruby knew better than to question the spirits or Arnold when he'd connected to them. She simply murmured *hau Tunkashila*— amen to the Creator—and wandered off to bed. She had a feeling Arnold would be up for quite some time. After all, he had work to do.

Arnold dumped the rest of his coffee onto the ground and walked back inside to a bureau in the living room. He gently slid the top drawer open and retrieved a bag made of softened elk hide. Long fringes hung down the belly of the bag. Ruby had beaded the back of the bag many years ago with multi-colored geometric patterns on a background of white.

Arnold reverently opened it and lifted the slender stem of the pipe, placing it to the side. He then grasped the bowl, polished to sheen and carved from a single piece of red pipestone. The magnificent carving fused the effigy of an eagle and a bear.

This old pipe had kept Arnold's family strongly connected, touching them all as it passed down to the next in line for many generations. His father gave Arnold the pipe when he got out of prison and redeemed his life. In prison, Arnold experienced visions that inspired him to choose a different path and he made a commitment to follow it. The pipe came with great responsibilities and he was about to fulfill one now.

On his knees, Arnold assembled the pipe and prayed as he did. He reached down for a pinch of the earthy tobacco and held it forward, high above his head. Arnold sang his prayers and lowered his fingers to load the pipe. The songs of thanks and pleading to the Creator carried on the wind and served as keys opening doors to the spirit world as they had done since ancient times. The brilliant stars above were an audience to Arnold's haunting songs and the pallid crescent moon served as host. As he struck a match to light the bowl, a trail of radiant light illuminated the dark sky as a star fell from its heavenly perch.

Many hours later, the morning sun split a crimson wedge along the horizon. Arnold was exhausted after his all-night vigil but satisfied as he sat on the porch in a lawn chair. He had prayed to keep Derek strong and courageous for what he faced and the trials that were sure to come. Arnold sang the same songs his father had sung for him while he was in prison. They were the same his grandfather sang for Arnold's father when he fought in the Pacific in World War II—the same songs sung by his ancestors to give protection for warriors about to engage in battle with other tribes or the U.S. Cavalry as they faced their greatest enemy, their own fears. He'd done what he could do and the rest was up to the spirits. It always was.

Ruby came up behind him and gently placed a warm hand on his shoulder. Ruby resembled a burrito wearing slippers, having had the Pendleton wrapped around her tightly.

"Do you want some breakfast?"

"No, I'm too tired, sweetheart. I'm going to bed."

They both watched in awe as the fiery orb rose from its nest on the prairie. Watching the birth of a new day never got old to the couple.

"Keep Derek in your thoughts, okay?"

Ruby nodded.

"He's going through something," Arnold continued. "Something big. I felt it all day yesterday and had to get the pipe out last night."

Ruby gave Arnold's shoulder a gentle squeeze in approval. She turned and headed to heat the stove. Arnold couldn't help thinking about the inipi ceremony with Derek. He hadn't been able to put his finger on it, but something powerful happened while they were in there. He had seen flashes of color. He heard the voice of a child. Someone had been in there with them …

Back in San Diego, Nina heard the door unlocking and turned to see a tormented shell of a man enter the house. Derek looked drained with red, puffy eyes. The girls squealed and came running to the door, gripping their dad's legs tightly. Derek looked down at them as if he saw them for the first time. He squeezed both girls tightly, desperately. Nina tingled with emotion as she watched the scene unfold.

"Are you okay honey?" she asked.

Derek only nodded as he picked up his luggage and walked upstairs in a stupor. Nina assumed the sales trip had been a tough one and decided she'd talk to him after he'd had a chance to un-pack and she could feed the girls. As she chopped a cucumber, her mind was a tempest, realizing this new sales circuit was a blow to Derek's ego, if not outright embarrassing. She vowed to treat him gently. She didn't want to argue tonight.

Derek walked upstairs and gingerly removed his jacket. His hands hurt like hell, but he focused on the angel statuette on his dresser. He removed his clothes and unpacked his suitcase, fre-quently looking back at the angelic figure clinging tightly to the little boy. Derek felt weak and hollowed out. He looked at his shredded hands and recognized his insides were the same. Torn. Damaged. Derek stepped into the shower not to just wash away the grime, but also the aching in his hands and his heart.

The next morning Derek was up early reviewing the projected sales figures he hadn't achieved. He knew his head hadn't been in the game lately. The sales he made were only replacement purchases of urgently needed broken equipment in the clinics he visited, sales that would have been made anyway. He would have some tap dancing to do once Sedgewick got the reports.

His thoughts turned to Skip and the monumental task ahead of apologizing for his stupidity and misplaced anger. Derek had shunned one of the only friends he had left, the one that had probably saved his job. The pill of pride he'd have to swallow seemed enormous, impossibly hard to choke down, but after what had happened in South Dakota, perhaps it was time to try. He looked at his watch and then punched the digits into his cell phone.

"Hi Derek," Skip answered flatly.

"Good morning Skip."

Derek knew Skip had tried his best to understand to his struggles, but even Skip had his limits. Derek did his best to be diplomatic and navigate the waters carefully. The two talked shop, giving each other updates on work, Sedgewick and sales numbers—or lack thereof. Skip warmed up and even tried to be a help, giving Derek the results of some research he had done that week on the needs of the small clinics in rural areas. Derek was ashamed that after the way he'd treated Skip, his friend had still gone out of his way for him. That reality spurred Derek to do what he needed to do.

"Skip, I wanted to thank you for what you did," he said with the rush of plunging into an icy pool.

"No big deal. I had some free time on my hands so I figured, what the hell," Skip said dismissively.

"No, not just that ... but everything. And for running interference for me with Sedgewick."

They both laughed at the unavoidable football reference.

"And thanks for always being my friend."

Skip began to say something but Derek wasn't finished and needed to say more before he lost nerve.

"I'm really sorry man. I was way out of line and dead wrong about what I said to you and Nina." Reliving the moments made Derek lower his head in shame. "Lately, I've been so ..."

"Don't worry about it Derek. Apology accepted." Skip replied. "Besides, Global Medix would suck more than I could stand if you got fired."

Just as Derek ended his call with Skip, Nina appeared in the doorway with a tired smile and wild hair. His heart leapt from his chest and he wanted to spill the recent events right there but thought better of it.

"I wanted to talk to you about your trip, but by the time I made it upstairs, you were already asleep."

"Oh. Well, yeah, I was pretty exhausted," Derek said while trying to hide the palms of his hands. He didn't want to have to explain what he didn't even understand himself. The two talked about the day's schedule and his upcoming travels, safely steering clear of the things that really mattered. Throughout the conversation, one idea gripped Derek: he *had* to run today.

With trembling hands, Derek laced up his shoes and noticed they didn't look so new anymore. He got dressed and gathered what he needed, feeling the gravity of moments to come. He decided to drive down to San Diego Bay and run along the marina. Derek's feet pounded out a steady cadence; the sea breeze and salty air rejuvenated him.

The sailboats bobbed up and down on the indigo water like toys, and the walkway around the marina was filled with activity. He saw street performers, artists, food vendors and pursed his lips in frustration at the crowds, realizing it was a Saturday. Kids recklessly darted across Derek's path as he tried to understand the pieces of urban art sculpture fixed along the water's edge like a frozen parade. The goliath of the U.S.S. Midway loomed in the distance, once a mighty warrior of the seas, now emasculated and converted to a tourist attraction.

Derek quickened his pace and felt good, but no buzzing sensations. He slowed his run to a jog and saw Dr. Parker walking arm in arm with his wife as she pushed a baby stroller. The other two tikes, both boys, walked closely in front of the couple and pointed at the boats in the harbor when they weren't taking playful swipes at each other.

"Well, if it isn't my favorite patient," Dr. Parker said cheerfully.

"And my favorite doctor," Derek remarked as he slowed to a walk and the two shook hands. "How are you, Fred?"

"Very well, thanks. Mary Beth and I decided to take the grandkids for the day and enjoy this fine weather."

Dr. Parker's wife smiled a greeting to Derek as she chased after the grandkids, now fixated on a large Dalmatian trotting by with his owner in tow.

"What on earth happened to you?" Dr. Parker said, suddenly wide-eyed as he stared at Derek's hands.

"Oh, um, I fell down in a parking lot the other day," Derek answered. He realized that sounded ridiculous and changed the story. "I stepped on some gum." Now the story made him look like an imbecile.

"Have you called my office for that follow up?" the doctor asked. "There are more tests we can run to see what's going on."

"Well, uh, I've been traveling a lot lately."

Dr. Parker looked skeptical.

"I'm fine, really," Derek said as he squirmed in his shoes.

Dr. Parker seemed unconvinced but his wife and the grand-kids were drifting away in a sea of people and he had to go, letting Derek off the hook.

Derek walked back to the car, enjoying the sunshine but feeling disappointed by the run. It was probably for the best that it was short and uneventful. What if he'd had the electric tingle or worse, the floating, with other people watching? Derek guessed perhaps that is why the phenomenon didn't happen this time—too many people around.

He quickly jumped into the car, paid the parking attendant and took off to find somewhere quiet to run. Finding wide open spaces without any people in San Diego on a Saturday seemed an impossible task. Derek headed east and out of town, determined to head to Arizona if needed. He had to run again today.

Nearly an hour later he pulled the car off the highway onto a smaller, isolated two-lane road and decided to take his chances. Minutes later he ran along the wide dirt apron that bordered the road. Sweat beaded on his forehead and the back of his throat burned. His brown skin shined like melted caramel under the hot sun. His ever-shrinking belly was lifting and dropping in rhythm with his feet. As Derek's muscles loosened and he got into his pace, the tingling returned. The internal buzz, the envelope of static electricity and the gentle pressure returned, lifting Derek off the ground. He knew what to do. He kept his pace despite the shock of the moment.

"Can you hear me, Cole?" Derek asked, eager to establish a connection.

"Yes, Daddy. I can hear you."

A lump planted itself inside Derek's parched throat.

"I'm so sorry we lost you," Derek offered, but could barely could speak the words. "I miss you every day. We all do." The moment was both fantastic and excruciating.

"I know. I've missed you all too. But you didn't lose me. I wasn't meant to stay."

"But it was unfair. You were with us such a short time," Derek said, trying to mask his rising anger at the cruel loss. "We loved you so much. And still do," he added. "How could you be taken from us?"

"All things pass in time. Whether a tree, a bird, or a person, all things will pass in time. This life is limited only by time. What you do with the moments is what matters."

Derek tried hard to catch his breath enough to respond, surprised that such wisdom came in the voice of child. "But you were here such a short time. You didn't get the chance to do anything with your moments."

"I loved. That's the best thing to do with moments we have. I tried to show it when I chose to leave so you and Mommy didn't have to make that choice."

A massive burden lifted from Derek's heart, one he'd been carrying since the moment Cole passed.

"You … chose?" Derek asked, trying to process the words.

"I chose."

Derek's head swirled and he tried with all his might to keep running and keep the conversation going. "Is that the reason you've come back? To tell me that?" He realized in that moment he didn't want redemption as much as he wanted Cole to stay and hoped Cole hadn't just now fulfilled his reason for returning. He clung to Cole in his heart, like a child to a blanket, and couldn't lose him again.

"I don't know why I've come back," Cole said.

Derek was panting and his pace fading.

"But I'm happy I'm here."

"Me too, Cole," Derek wheezed. "I'm so happy. Can I tell the others?"

Derek wasn't sure why he'd asked, but needed to. He looked down at the weeds and wildflowers several feet below him.

"No, Daddy. I'm not sure why I've come back, but I do know I've only come back to be with you. The others don't need me now."

Derek was surprised by the answer and even more by the explanation.

"How long will you stay with me?"

"Until I'm called home again," Cole answered with the sweetest timbre in his voice. "I'll have to go back when he decides."

Derek had a feeling who "he" was.

"Cole, I can't run anymore," Derek uttered between gasps.

"I know, Daddy," Cole answered playfully. "You better stop for now. You're getting heavy."

Derek thought that statement odd but would have to explore later. He'd collapse if he didn't stop running. Before he slowed his pace and lost the connection, he had to say it. "I love you, Cole. I love you so much."

"I love you too, Daddy." Cole's answered as his voice faded.

Derek staggered to a stop as his tears mingled with sweat. His legs were like lead but his heart soared as he walked the rest of the way back to the car. This was really happening. Derek no longer thought this was a hallucination. A real connection had opened between him and his lost son. Neither of them understood why or how long it would last.

He remembered his time in church as a kid with the Sorensens. Derek learned all things are possible through God, but never heard a sermon about something like this. For certain, something had shifted and a tunnel had opened, not just between

Cole and Derek, but within Derek himself. He pondered this surreal and emotional situation on the drive home and in the midst of
it all, one thing was absolutely certain and inescapable—Derek
couldn't wait until he could run again.

When he got home, Nina and the girls were laughing as they tried
to follow a yoga program on TV. He saw Bailey and Hannah strike
the warrior pose and then downward dog, thinking how lucky the
girls were to have a mother like theirs. Derek wanted so badly to
tell them his secret, but he also wanted to honor Cole's edict. Nina
noticed him and smiled. Her hair was even more curled from the
heat of exertion. She was beautiful and Derek realized how lucky
he was too.

"Break time, girls," Nina said to moans from Hannah and
Bailey. She walked over to Derek and the fine layer of perspiration
made her face glow. Impulsively, Derek reached up and brushed
her hair from her face—a long-absent loving gesture that surprised
them both.

"My God, you're a beautiful woman, Nina," Derek said and
then looked away as if it wasn't his place to say it anymore.

Nina touched his jaw and shifted his head back.

"And I'm *yours*, Derek. All yours."

Derek reached with his deeply shredded hand and held hers.
Though it shot bolts of pain up his arm, he gently squeezed her
hand in acknowledgement. He needed to repair so many bridges in
his life, but he knew the most important bridge was the one that
would lead him back to Nina's heart. The task seemed daunting
and shrouded in doubt.

"I better get upstairs and pack for tomorrow," Derek said.

Nina forced a smile and went back to the girls.

The next day, Derek drove to the airport like a madman. Running late for his flight, he kept glancing at his watch as if willing the time to slow down. The shower he took this morning was negated by the clammy sweat collecting in his armpits and around his collar.

"Go!" Derek yelled as he beeped at the car in front of him.

The driver of the red BMW casually applied makeup in her rearview mirror. She actually gave herself a once over before closing her makeup case and readjusting her mirror. To Derek, days like this made him suspect the world had conspired to hold him back and derail his best laid plans.

After being in the security line behind an elderly woman with a light blue beehive hairdo who had liquids, gels and illegal metal objects in her purse, Derek finally made it into the concourse. He walked quickly past a poster promoting a casino for one of the local Indian tribes and thought of his own tribe. Derek often wondered if he'd ever solve the mystery of his roots. He squirmed every time he explained the "yeah-I'm-Indian-but-don't-know-what-tribe" routine to skeptical looks. He felt loosely linked to every tribe he'd learned about, but not really connected to any of them. It was a sense of traveling abroad for many years, waiting eagerly to return home but not knowing what country home actually was. A ship without a harbor. An Indian without a tribe. How sad.

Derek made it to the gate just in time to be the last passenger to board. His cell phone rang but he decided not to answer it and got settled into his seat instead. The sixty-something woman next to him smelled like she'd marinated herself in perfume. She had a hairdo teased out to its limits and held in place, or rather imprisoned, with Aqua Net.

Once he was squared away, he looked at his phone and saw that Sarah had left him a text message. She was interested in buying a few pieces of new equipment. Derek relaxed, knowing the best sales trips were ones where the sale was done before ever leaving home. The fragrant woman next to him took his demeanor for sociability. She insisted on knowing Derek's life story and sharing hers as well. Like a fly at a picnic, the woman was relentless. A few minutes into the flight, Derek felt disoriented by her overpowering fumes. He could see her mouth moving but he could no longer make sense of her words.

When their plane arrived at the tiny airport, Derek quickly exited security and spotted Sarah waiting for him in her hot pink Crocs. She smiled, waved and ended her cell phone call. The term *motivation* didn't quite capture Sarah's energy and focus. She reminded Derek of a hummingbird in scrubs.

"I guess you want that equipment pretty bad," Derek said, quickly regretting his worst-ever sales line.

"Oh, well yeah, but that's not why I came out here. How are you doing?"

They both knew what she meant. Derek had been in a quandary since he'd spilled the beans to Sarah, but now compelled to tell her no more after Cole's guidance.

"Doing great," Derek said a bit too enthusiastically. "Everything is better now."

Sarah was obviously trying to read Derek and her curiosity bore a hole through him. He owed her something after her willingness to listen, but before he could give it, Sarah dropped the inquisition and shrugged.

"If you say it's alright, then it's alright."

Derek breathed a sigh of relief.

Sarah continued, "Now, about that equipment ..."

Later that day Derek was back at his motel room. He changed from his business clothes to running gear and stretched his legs. He reflected on the day and though it had been a business success, Derek's mind was elsewhere. He thought of Sarah and Arnold in that they were both so strong and rooted in their culture, proud of who they were, where they came from and lived their lives with the dignity of that knowledge.

"Is knowing what tribe you are really that important?" he remembered asking Sarah. She had looked at him as if he'd asked her what planet they were currently visiting.

"Only if you want to know who you really are?" she answered. The response had intrigued Derek, but also deflated him since he might never know the answer.

Derek tried to call Arnold but the phone just kept ringing. He vaguely remembered a ceremony Arnold had to attend on another reservation and made a mental note to call him on his next visit.

He put his thumbs into his waistband to straighten his shorts and realized how loose they were. How much weight had he lost? He knew that he had felt much better since he started running, but this melting away was a very pleasant side effect. In the mirror he noticed that he didn't look like such a blob anymore.

Derek, more than ever, wanted this run to be in privacy. He trotted along the two-lane highway until he saw a dirt road break away and decided to follow. The rhythmic crunch of his steps on the gravel coupled with the puffs of dust rising with each beat. The sky was a brilliant blue canvas with a few chubby clouds hung for contrast. Grasshoppers clicked. Golden prairie grass swayed and pulsed in the wind.

He licked his salty lips and accelerated, getting into the zone he sought. Liquid electricity raced through his veins as steady vibrations increased throughout his body. Derek suddenly shot several feet off the ground, which took his breath away.

"Hi Daddy!" Cole's bright voice greeted him.

"Hi Cole!" Derek said. He overflowed with questions.

"Can I ask you something, Cole?"

"Yes. I think that's why I'm here," Cole answered.

"What happened to my birth parents?"

"I don't know," Cole replied.

"What tribe am I from?"

Again, Cole said, "I don't know. I'm sorry I don't know these things, Daddy."

"How can I make things better?" Derek begged.

"What things?" Cole asked.

"What things? Everything. My life, my job, letting go of the past. *Everything.*" Derek felt like a dam had ruptured within him and the words spilled out.

"What is that, Daddy?" Cole asked. Derek spied a box turtle shuffling across the road and realized Cole could see through his eyes.

"It's a turtle," Derek said, slightly annoyed at the shift in Cole's focus.

"I never saw one. He's slow. It might take him all day to get across the road," Cole said with amusement.

"Yeah, but he'll get there eventually."

"Uh huh," Cole agreed.

Derek grinned. Cole had the childlike perspective in having never seen a turtle and yet wisely used it to answer Derek's question.

"So, you're saying I should have patience?"

"Uh huh. Just like you tell Bailey and Hannah to practice and be patient in schoolwork or ballet or anything they do."

Derek saw all the times in his life he'd tried to make quick fixes of messes that were long times in the making. When it came to relationships, jobs or most things he did, Derek took the path of least resistance. If it became hard, he let it be and moved on to something else. Or ran away to something else. That way of thinking hadn't done him much good lately. Had it ever?

Pappa Don had always told him anything worth doing was worth the patience to do it right. Derek always considered that meant repairing the house or fixing a car, but perhaps it meant much more. He thought of the best things in a person's life and realized they all took practice and patience to build—a family, a community, a career … or a life. And none of them happened at the click of a mouse or snap of a finger.

Yet, how many countless commercials had he seen in countless nights on hotel TVs promising instant fixes, quick remedies, the next pill or procedure, and get rich quick schemes? How had he missed learning this lesson: that precious things take patience to grow?

"I'll have to work on this," Derek offered. "It's not my strongest skill."

"Have you seen a shooting star?" Cole asked excitedly.

"Of course," Derek said trying to catch his breath and fight the side stitch that had started.

"They're one of my favorite things!" Cole declared.

Derek thought it odd that Cole would shift from a turtle to a shooting star.

"They travel so far, so very far and in the last second, they burn so bright, don't they? That long journey led to that pretty flash you see, that pretty flash you remember forever."

Derek got this one. He had always just wanted the flash and to forgo the long journey it took to create it.

Lost in the conversation, Derek suddenly found he was over a pasture and sailing right over a farmer's fence and a small tree. The flying was euphoric, exhilarating and added a dimension of pure wonder to the already amazing reality of communicating with his lost son. On the ground below, he saw constellations of yellow wildflowers rushing past and then crossed over a small pond, covered with dancing crystals of sunlight.

"I like this, Daddy." Cole said softly.

"Me too, Cole," Derek said. "Me too."

Back at the motel, Derek stepped out of the shower and studied his mangled hands. Deep pink rips were edged by wrinkly pale skin. The cuts were healing. Derek was starving after the run, one of the longest yet. He heard his phone ringing and wrapped his towel around him and walked out to get it.

"This is Derek," he said.

"Way to go my man!" the happy voice boomed.

"What? Skip, is that you?"

"Sedgewick freaked over the big order you placed today," Skip replied. He was pumped, but Derek had forgotten all about the sale during his run with Cole.

"You're back in the good graces of the Gipper."

"That's great, Skip," Derek said while he adjusted his towel. "Thanks for letting me know."

The corporate world of Global Medix, like an alien world, now seemed so far away. Derek didn't miss the bland furniture, the cool blue walls some designer said was good for employee focus or the sanitized stainless steel bathrooms that always smelled like ammonia—though it had been an escape for so long. Now he thoroughly enjoyed the smell of pine and sage, the feel of sun on his skin as he ran, the open spaces, and most of all, this precious time with Cole.

CHAPTER 8

THE TICKET COUNTER at the small airport was log-jammed with young men wearing red and white track suits of a college basketball team. The cacophony of cell phone conversations, gossip, trash-talking, laughter, slurping drinks and cutting up only grew louder when the coach turned his back to sort out ticketing issues with the agent.

Derek looked furtively at his watch and his blood pressure rose. Again, the powers that be seemed to have doomed him. Derek closed his eyes and took a deep breath. He imagined the turtle slowly, methodically and with great purpose heading to the other side of the dirt road. He saw Nina and the girls in his mind. Derek opened his eyes again. The college team and the chaos around them were gone.

"May I help you?" the gate agent asked.

The puddle-jumper airplane, like a cork in a Jacuzzi, got tossed mercilessly as it fought its way through a storm front. The situation got worse when the flight attendant dumped a plastic cup of tomato juice down the front of Derek's shirt.

"I am so sorry, sir," the flustered flight attendant offered as her hand dabbed at Derek's shirt like a chicken pecking dough.

"That's okay," Derek tried to mean it. "It'll just look like I was a stabbing victim when I get home to my family."

The flight attendant immediately burst into tears.

"Or I wrestled with a ketchup bottle," Derek quickly offered trying his best to be funny, "and lost."

She smiled through her sniffles.

"Seriously, it's perfectly fine. I hated this shirt anyway so ... thanks."

This got a laugh from the flight attendant as well as a few passengers. She walked away but returned with more napkins and some soda water.

"Thank you for being so patient. My daughter is home sick with the flu. I got called last minute for this roller coaster flight and now this," she said as she pointed at Derek's shirt. "I feel terrible."

The two chatted for a moment until a passenger in the back, who puked his guts out, rang for her. Poor lady. Derek felt better now that he'd cut her a break and realized how powerful this patience thing was. It all seemed to work out for the best. After all, he had indeed hated this shirt.

The rest of the journey home Derek reflected on the upcoming week. No trips and a busy schedule would leave little time to run. He already missed Cole and wondered if he couldn't duck out for a bit or call in sick. He reconsidered, realizing he was just now coming back into the good graces of the Gipper and didn't want to cause any more trouble or further endanger his job.

Derek got home late from the airport and quietly put his keys on the hook in the kitchen and tip-toed upstairs, leaving the lights off. He set his suitcase down and decided to unpack in the morning. As he undressed, Derek looked at Nina's slender body melted into the covers and mattress, bathed in the amber light from the alarm clock. Her hair cascaded around her shoulders and onto the bed like an ebony waterfall. Derek spied Nina's delicate toes peeking out below the comforter, her arm and hand draped gracefully over her forehead like a 1930's exasperated starlet from the big screen.

Derek reflected on his lesson of patience and cowered inside thinking of how patient Nina had been with him for the last year— actually their whole relationship. Nina never forced Derek's emotions out into the open against his will but simply invited them to appear in their own time. He reached down and tenderly pushed the hair away from her ear and kissed it.

"I love you, Nina," he whispered, and stepped into the bathroom and quietly shut the door.

The sun had crawled out of its nest the next morning and sat squarely above the trees while Derek sat in the parking lot sipping the last of his espresso. He was delaying his entry back into the halls of Global Medix as the radio droned on about the latest bloodbath on Wall Street and a beached whale in New Jersey. Derek watched two sparrows flying together playfully and thought of Cole. Glancing at his car's clock he confirmed it was time to go.

Derek walked through the main doors and headed for Skip's office. He knocked on Skip's open door just in time to see his friend shoot an easy three-pointer from across the room.

"Do you ever sleep?" Derek asked, noting a grease-stained pizza box on a distant corner of Skip's desk.

"Why sleep when there's work to be done?" Skip stood and the two shook hands and embraced, slapping backs so it wasn't weird. Skip cleared his desk of the remnants of his solo dinner and got caught up on the business at hand. In short, Sedgewick was pleased, sales were up and the world inside the pale blue walls was going well.

"Did you always want to do this for a living?" Derek asked, breaking the silence surrounding their review of some new medical equipment.

"Do what?" Skip asked as he skimmed paperwork.

"This. You know, medical equipment sales."

Skip looked up with a sly grin. "I wanted to do whatever earned me good money. This seemed to fit the bill."

Derek's face turned sour. He hadn't always wanted to do this. But then again, he didn't know what he would do if he wasn't doing this. He had vague, starry wishes but nothing solid came to mind. He looked out the window at the manicured grass and flowers flanking the parking lot. In the tree near his car perched those two sparrows again, sitting peacefully together on a low-hanging branch.

"Well, the Chief has returned from the warpath," Sedgewick gushed as he walked into the office uninvited. His toupee looked luminescent and more plastic than usual in the morning's light.

Derek rolled his eyes at Skip and turned around to greet his boss. "Morning, Mr. Sedgewick." Derek reluctantly shook Sedgewick's sweaty hand and noticed his boss's toupee sitting slightly further back on his head than it should be, like the baseball cap on a tired trucker after a long haul.

"You've been doing a great job out there and I'm happy to see you're still part of the team."

"Me too, sir," Derek said with a sideways glance to the man responsible for his continued employment. Skip nodded and winked.

"Well since you're both in here ... hot damn, Derek! You lose weight?"

Derek attempted to answer but Sedgewick rolled on.

"Anyways, since you're both here, I'll go ahead and tell you," Sedgewick said.

Skip beamed.

Sedgewick rocked on his heels, which meant he had an announcement. "Gordon Travis is retiring this month so there will be a place on the varsity team again," he said with a hand clap for emphasis.

Derek wasn't following and his vacant look said so.

"For you," Sedgewick continued, "I'm offering Houston, Phoenix and Denver back, Derek."

Derek felt like a rabbit snared in a net. After several moments of awkward silence, he stammered a response. "Well, I uh ... I appreciate the offer, but I'm actually feeling good about where I am now."

Sedgewick's smile drained from his face like sidewalk chalk in the rain. So did Skip's.

"What are you talking about, Derek? This is prime real estate, son. This is where the players play." Sedgewick looked at Skip as if willing him to talk some sense into his stupid friend. Skip's blank look offered no solace to Sedgewick.

"I'm getting to know my clients and their needs," Derek said. It was true and he hoped this appeal to business sense would sway the boss. What Derek really saw in his mind was exchanging first class tickets, five star hotels, fancy meals and much more money for puddle-jumping planes, roadside motels with squeaky beds, crappy food—and time with Cole. Derek wanted none of it.

"I can't do it, sir." Derek wanted to say he wouldn't do it, but caught himself. Sedgewick looked shocked. Skip looked devastated. But Derek held firm. Sedgewick mumbled something incoherent and left Skip's office shaking his head. Derek turned to Skip who looked out the window for answers, clearly disgusted.

"What was that about?" Skip asked, seemed more hurt than angry. "I've been in Sedgewick's ear about getting your territories back since he shafted you and here you have it offered with a silky bow ... and you say no?"

"Listen, Skip, I appreciate your effort, really." Derek wanted so badly to tell his friend the truth. "I'm sorry man, but I just can't. But thanks. Seriously."

The next week was monotonous and bleak. He was torn, happy to be reunited with Skip but feeling like a captive inside the catacombs of Global Medix. Derek had tried to use the time wisely and made countless phone calls to potential clients, read up on the latest equipment specs and generally made himself look like an asset to the company. But like a kid counting down the days until Christmas, he anxiously counted the moments until he could hit the road again and be with Cole.

He spent every lunch hour on the treadmill at the fitness center, trying to get in better shape so he could run longer to spend more time with Cole. Luckily, he never floated, but a few times he had the gentle buzz, which was comforting.

The running came at a cost. Each night he nursed wounds suffered from the long runs. He iced achy knees, did blister repair, and one night Derek nearly jumped out of his skin as the hot water from the shower washed over his chafed nipples. He wished he'd have listened to Harvey at the running store. The skin on Derek's inner thighs seemed like they'd been rubbed raw with a belt sander and sported glowing, red welts. His knees nearly buckled when the hot water hit that area.

When he wasn't working or running, Derek relished more time with the girls and Nina. The family went to Chuck E. Cheese and everyone seemed to genuinely enjoy themselves. It had been so long since they had. Derek was always fascinated that Hannah loved going to the place. She claimed that the man in the Chuck E. Cheese costume gave her the creeps and she cried every time he came near. On the drive home Derek had a flash of insight that blew him away; his little girl loved the games and pizza enough to face her fears.

"What is it, Derek?" Nina asked when she noticed Derek stopped singing along with the family to the Sponge Bob soundtrack.

"Oh, I just remembered something really important," Derek said. "Something I'd forgotten."

Derek finally headed back to South Dakota. Getting on the over-sold commuter flight from Denver evoked the drama of making it onto the last chopper out before the fall of Saigon. People argued and screamed at the gate, demanding a seat. Derek sympathized. He would have been engrossed in the fray had his airline status not secured him a seat. He too was willing to fight to get back to South Dakota. After all, his son waited to join him there on his next run.

The tiny clown car he drove was the last one at the rental place and seemed like it would tip over in the wind. And it was ca-nary yellow. He couldn't have cared less as he focused on the road ahead. After checking in at the motel, his clothes flew off him and out of his bag until he appeared out of the stumbling blur like Superman from a phone booth, dressed and ready for the run ahead.

An hour later, Cole and Derek were laughing hysterically. Derek had just swallowed a bug while flying twenty feet off the ground. He had made several dry heave gags, first as a joke but the last few were genuine, which made it even funnier to both. Derek shook his head as sweat flew in every direction.

"Well, that was probably better than lunch at the motel," Derek said.

Cole giggled.

"The week was miserable without you," Derek professed.

"Why miserable?"

"Because I had to wait to be with you. I couldn't get away to run anywhere without people." Derek thought it was obvious.

"But you could have enjoyed the week anyway."

Derek didn't follow.

"You shouldn't have to wait for good things. Life is now and good things are all around."

A group of rotund cows casually looked up at a sweaty Indian guy gliding over a stand of trees and continued to chew their cud.

"I guess that makes sense."

"Remember when you were a boy and went to the county fair? You waited in line for over an hour in the hot sun to ride the big red and white thingy."

Derek remembered the sweltering heat that made him and his cotton candy melt as he waited to ride the "red and white thingy," the Rockin' Rocket. It had been a long, brutal wait for mere moments of fun.

"Imagine you were there again and didn't have to wait. Would you rather stand in line waiting and waiting for that minute of fun or just keep going to the front and riding as many times as you want?"

Derek grunted his understanding.

"You don't have to wait in line," Cole said. "This is the ride. Life is now."

Derek reflected on how much of his life had been spent waiting for the good things. Waiting to find his birth parents. Waiting for the bullying to stop. Waiting for a promotion, for retirement. Waiting to heal. It seemed like he'd always been waiting for something good, something to change, and missed out on so many moments he could have made so much better. He laughed inwardly pondering how much we wait and the longer we wait the more expectation and pressure we place on the result being good. After all, if we've waited so long, it has to be good, right?

Derek remembered Sedgewick's vacation to Costa Rica last year. His boss had bragged about it for months, saying how perfect it would be, how sunny and relaxing. The vacation came and it rained the entire week. Instead of making the best of the vacation, Sedgewick returned bitter, claiming he got ripped off.

Derek saw how many conditions and expectations he had put on his life and his own happiness. He thought of Skip and how hard he worked and saved for a perfect someday, while missing out on so many other opportunities. Skip didn't date much, didn't have a hobby and never vacationed. In fact, he didn't do much except work. How could Skip choose to live like that and delay happiness for so long when his parents were taken so suddenly? Derek felt ashamed, realizing he'd been doing the same thing.

"So you're saying we should be happy now and live all of our moments in life, not just wait around for the good ones?"

"This is what I know. We should savor the gift and honor the time because the ride won't last. And when we have to get off, it seems too soon and it's sad for everyone."

The words dropped like bombs on Derek and made a deep impact. Maybe the reason Cole came back was to finally teach Derek this valuable lesson, one he'd ignored for so long. Derek made a private vow to work on this idea and to *savor the gift and honor the time.*

He recalled a poem he'd read and loved years ago that read: *Captive soul behind frigid bars, why do you stay caged? The key to freedom and freedom's bliss, is not in your mournful tears. It has always been ... in your hand.* He had read that poem countless times, but now that line made sense—it had meaning. Derek chose to release himself and be happy in this moment, without limits, without condition or timelines. He could feel his heart get lighter. A smile spread across his face like a sunrise. Truly joyful in this moment, he closed his eyes.

"Watch out, Daddy!"

Derek's eyes flew open in panic but it was too late. He got a face full of what looked like white paint as a trio of doves flew over him ... but he realized it wasn't white paint.

Arnold Kills Straight pulled back the curtain of the kitchen sink window. "Looks like rain," he said casually and continued peeling potatoes. Ruby dug through the closet as a board game came tumbling out, spilling its pieces across the floor. "What the heck are you doing, woman?"

"Ah, here it is," Ruby said, ignoring Arnold and triumphantly holding up an odd-shaped case. She lovingly stroked the surface and wiped the dust off with her hand. "It's been awhile but I wanted to play something tonight since we're having company."

Arnold continued peeling. He'd gotten a call from Derek earlier in the day. Arnold invited him to dinner and was happy he'd accepted. He'd missed the young man and wanted to see how he'd been. Derek said he'd be in meetings all day and not to expect him until after seven. As the sun set, a rap at the front door announced Derek's arrival.

Ruby opened the door and squeezed him like a long-lost relative, which seemed to surprise Derek. Arnold smiled warmly and shook Derek's hand. "Hau Kola. It's good to see you again."

"Hau to you too Kola," Derek attempted the traditional greeting with added English. Ruby took Derek's hand and guided him into the house, shuffling forward in furry slippers.

"How were your meetings today?" Ruby asked.

"Way too long. I talked so much today, my throat is raw." Derek held his hand to his neck.

"You need some medicine," Arnold said as he walked to the kitchen and searched through the cabinet.

"Oh no, it's okay, Arnold. I'm not sick or anything," Derek countered.

Arnold stopped his search and looked at Derek. "Medicine isn't just for when you're sick. It's to keep you from getting sick in the first place."

Derek's furrowed brow showed his confusion.

"Look, medicine to us isn't just Allegra or Motrin. Or that Viagra," Arnold said.

Ruby giggled and shook her head.

"It's anything and everything that keeps us strong enough—spiritually, mentally and physically—to be our best and deal with the world around us. It can be taking a walk, getting enough sleep, being with your kids, going to sweatlodge or anything else that serves you in a good way," Arnold explained. He continued his search as he talked. "The keys are to first know what your medicine is and the second is to use it. It keeps you walking in balance in this crazy ol' world we live in now. Ah, there it is." Arnold held up a plastic baggy with several dark brown, craggy roots. "Bear root."

Ruby nodded approval.

"Here, chew on this and swallow the juice," Arnold said.

Reluctantly, Derek bit into the woody root and chewed. After a few minutes, his mouth tingled and started feeling slightly numb. So did his throat. This was better than popping a Halls drop—and tasted better too.

When it was time for dinner, Arnold brought out grand platters holding delectable treats. One held a salad of mixed greens, beets, walnuts and goat cheese; the other a small pile of fingerling potatoes coated in sage, butter and sea salt and the last held pieces of buffalo schnitzel with a balsamic drizzle.

Ruby tittered at Derek's surprise. "He's always watching those cooking shows on TV," she explained. "Don't know if he's Emeril Kills Straight or Arnold LeGasse."

"It's my secret hobby," Arnold confessed and shrugged his shoulders. "What can I say?" The tall Indian with a plaid shirt, wranglers, cowboy boots and braids couldn't have seemed more an unlikely chef of such delicate cuisine. "I figured you might appreciate it more than my friends around here." Arnold pouted and leaned forward. "They call it fancy food."

The three had a friendly dinner over perfect food and talked about the goings on in the local community and Derek's job. Derek wanted to learn more about Lakota tribal history and both Arnold and Ruby happily obliged. The last course was brought out by Ruby and she set a bowl of bright purple goo on the table and doled it out into smaller porcelain bowls. Derek looked at Arnold with curious eyes.

"This is Ruby's department," Arnold said. "I don't mess with perfection."

Derek tried the thick, lumpy sauce and it was heavenly.

"Wow! What is this?" Derek gushed with purpled teeth.

"It's a traditional dish called wojapi or fruits of the earth pudding," Ruby answered. "It's mashed up chokecherries, buffalo berries and blueberries. And some other stuff too," she winked. "Our people have been eating this since forever."

"I can see why," Derek lifted another spoonful to his mouth. "Medicine, huh?"

"You got it, brother," Arnold chimed.

Ruby put on some fresh coffee and migrated to another room, returning with her gleaming banjo. Derek settled back into the couch and sipped his coffee while Ruby sat on the edge of a well-worn overstuffed chair. She started picking and grinning. The upbeat staccato of the banjo burst with playful energy and filled Derek's heart with nostalgia he couldn't place. Maybe his birth parents played this when he was a baby. Arnold bopped his head and kept making faces at Ruby that she teasingly returned.

After the impromptu concert, Derek and Arnold walked out onto the porch to look at the stars and talk. Derek shoved his hands deep into his pockets, feeling the inner pressure of wanting to share his experiences with Arnold but not able.

"Gosh, you can actually see it out here," Derek said, nodding his chin skyward to the Milky Way.

"It's beautiful, isn't it?" Arnold replied between sips of his coffee.

"Whoa!" Derek pointed up. "Did you see that?"

Arnold nodded at the shooting star.

"We don't see those much where I live." Derek reflected on Cole's words and the journey the star must have made.

Arnold pointed upward. "Check that out."

Derek looked up at the faint flashing of an airliner at high altitude.

"We don't see many of those where I live," Arnold joked.

"That's nothing special." Derek waved his hand.

"Wouldn't know," Arnold said as a matter of fact.

"You've never been on an airliner?" Derek was incredulous thinking of the countless flights and millions of miles he'd flown. It was routine for him.

"Never been on any kind of airplane." Arnold squinted at the passing jet. "All the same, I always thought it would be neat, you know, cruising up there like a bird or some kind of spirit." Arnold watched the aircraft, cutting a moonlit contrail across the sky. "Just never had a reason to do it and at this age, don't figure I ever will."

How long it had been since he looked at flying that way. It was just part of his job and a boring part at that. It was a time to catch up on work or sleep. Derek couldn't remember the last time he'd more than glanced out of the airplane window. He presumed everyone had been on a plane before and suddenly felt guilty. Arnold and Ruby had so much less in means than Derek and yet seemed so much happier. Who was really more fortunate?

"How have you been lately?" Arnold asked Derek.

"Oh, doing pretty good." Derek held back what he'd wanted to say and offered the standard line instead.

"I've been thinking about you lately and keeping you in our prayers," Arnold said. "I felt like you were going through some-thing big lately, like a disturbance."

Derek's heart rate jumped.

"What, like the force?" Derek tried to cover up feeling exposed with the joke about Star Wars. Could Arnold really know what had been going on?

"Yeah, something like that," Arnold chuckled.

"No, everything is good. I've just been working hard," Derek didn't want to lie to Arnold but had no other choice.

Arnold sensed Derek was holding back. After all, Derek looked like he carried the weight of a waterlogged Pendleton blanket, but he knew not to press such things and let it go. It wasn't his battle to fight. All he could do was keep Derek in his prayers and promised himself that he would.

"I could never get tired of this," Derek panted as he zipped over a rusted out propane tank the next day.

"Me neither," Cole added. "Weeeeee!"

Derek's legs pumped like pistons and the warm air and fragrance of wet hay filled his lungs. He rotated his head around, enjoying the scenery, the experience. These moments.

"Cole, you said life is now. But is there another life after this?"

"Of course, Daddy!" Cole said. "How else could I be here?"

Derek had always wanted to believe this. Now that it was confirmed, he decided to leave it alone. Discussing heaven seemed too big of a subject to tackle right now.

"When you say life is now, what about all the other things that can get in the way of now?"

"Like what?"

"Well, like other stuff. Disappointment, fear or pain. I don't know. The past."

Cole's silence gave Derek time to ponder his own statement and then support his position.

"My pain and anger have become sources of strength for me. They've kept me afloat all these years. They're what helped me fight the feelings of being abandoned, bullied or scared." Derek pumped his legs even harder, convinced these emotions were useful to him.

"No, Daddy," Cole whispered, "They're what keep you below the surface of the water. They've made you heavy," Cole answered softly. "So heavy."

"What do you mean, *heavy*?" Derek wondered.

"I tried to lift you before but I couldn't because of all you carry. It's too much."

Derek thought back to the stumbles and crashes when he started running and realized Cole had been trying to lift him up, to talk with him even then. So much of his life had been spent keeping score, holding grudges and carrying the pieces of his guilt and shame, shaping them into what he falsely believed was armor. Now he realized that all he had done was forge his own shackles.

"What do I do?" Derek asked.

"Forgive," Cole said without hesitation. "Forgive and put down your heavy load. You can't understand life is now if you don't."

"What? Forgive my birth parents, my tormentors in school, all the people who've wronged me?" Derek was indignant. "They don't deserve it!" he snarled.

"Yes, forgive them, not just for their sake but for yours."

"I don't know," Derek gasped, "I don't know if I ever can I can't ever forget what they've done."

"You won't forget. But you can forgive. And when you can do that, you can forgive the one you need to forgive the most—yourself."

Derek knew this weight well. It was his penance, his self-inflicted torture, to carry the shame of what he'd done to his mom.

How could he possibly let that go? Bad people who did wrong should be punished, right? What justice could there be if he set that burden down? He realized even prisoners had terms. They served their time and were released. Derek never had plans of paroling his enemies or himself, let alone granting a release date.

Derek considered the rage he'd carried toward his transgressors and how that rage had backfired. Had carrying this self-loathing and shame made him a better husband, a better father? A better anything? On the contrary, it had made him weak, afraid, skittish toward those who loved him and paranoid toward life or anything good in it. It had indeed made him heavy. Who was he really punishing by carrying this anger? Derek realized it hadn't just been himself. It had been Nina, his girls, his friends, everyone he loved. It always had been that way and he saw it now.

Derek turned his face to the sun, reached out his arms to release the inner rot he'd carried so long. He deeply breathed in the fresh air, laced with the sweet scent of fallen rain. He breathed in this time with Cole. He breathed in life itself. Derek flew higher and higher, above the trees and the power lines. He looked down and saw he had to be a hundred feet off the ground! Derek wasn't scared though, not anymore. *Life was now.*

CHAPTER 9

"MR. STONE SHOULD be here shortly," one of the senior board members announced as everyone in the room stiffened. The room was stocked with fresh fruit and pastries, but everyone just nervously sipped their coffee and spoke in hushed tones. Derek and Skip were attending this board meeting to promote some new equipment for Global Medix. The rest of the board and ancillary players were present, but everyone waited on Mr. Stone. Nothing could happen without him and everyone, including Mr. Stone, knew it.

"This guy's a real piece of work," Skip mumbled to Derek as his thumbs texted furiously on his phone. "He used to be a big shot CEO of Chase-Parker and then bailed out when the waters got rough. He took a huge severance, stock options, the works. The guy's richer than King Solomon."

"Then why would he sit on the board of a hospital?" Derek asked.

"Well, I guess the guy's bored. He's a first-class SOB and I've heard talk that he got tired of having no one to terrorize and bully. His wife left him. His kids hate him. He's got no one left but us," Skip said with a smirk.

Mr. Stone walked in wearing a tailored three-piece suit, a Rolex and carrying an Italian leather briefcase. He also carried with him an air of hostility that immediately affected the room. The board members already looked glum and defeated.

"Gentlemen, shall we get started?" Mr. Stone asked, ignoring the presence of three women in the room. He knew the answer and didn't bother looking up as everyone nodded.

The meeting clipped along briskly with Mr. Stone peppering the audience with backhanded insults, quips, grunts of disapproval and never missing an opportunity to prove his superiority over the others. Despite Mr. Stone's money and influence, it seemed he needed the board much more than the board needed him.

"What were the profit margins last quarter?" Mr. Stone grilled the financial guru even though he already knew the answer.

"Um ..." Mr. Wilson shuffled nervously through the papers, "Down two percent."

Mr. Stone furrowed his eyebrow. "We can see your idea to increase doctor time with patients cut into how many patients could be seen in a day, which cut into profits." Mr. Stone glared at a chubby board member with wire-rimmed glasses and a tenuous expression. "In retrospect, we can see that idea was rather stupid as I said it would be."

"Well, sir, we *are* a hospital providing patient care and we thought perhaps ..."

"First and always, we are a *business!*" Mr. Stone barked. "We don't pay our bills or our shareholders with warm fuzzies and good feelings. Fortunately you have at least *one* board member that remembers that fact."

Everyone in the room knew who he meant.

Derek wondered about the process that shaped Mr. Stone into the person he is. How could someone have achieved so much and yet achieved so little in the end? Fancy things, a big bank account and career success seemed a poor substitute for other less tangible things like happiness or even love. Mr. Stone was perhaps the richest man Derek had been around and at the same time, the most miserable. The man spoke acid, breathed hatred and sent out vibes of pure negativity. It was no wonder his wife left him, his kids couldn't stand him—and neither could anyone else.

Derek refused to believe Mr. Stone had always been this way. After all, the man at one time had a family. Maybe Mr. Stone had friends at one time as well. Derek guessed everyone had their limit. His curiosity turned to shame as he realized the likeness he shared with this hollowed out curmudgeon. He wondered what Nina's limit was and anxiously chewed on his pen, hoping he hadn't already pushed her past it.

When Nina got home that night, she had a bag of groceries in her arms, so she shut the door behind her with her foot. Her senses were overwhelmed with divine aromas.

"Derek?" she called out.

Derek walked out of the kitchen and whispered, "I'm in here," and motioned for her to follow.

Nina entered the kitchen and set the groceries down on the one clear space on the breakfast bar. Derek, wearing her apron, had a colorful confusion filling the kitchen. There was spilled pepper and breadcrumbs, open containers, and a scattering of chopped vegetables. The oven radiated heat and glorious smells. Nina stood there, stunned in silence.

"I put the kids to bed already so it's just us," he said like a happy conspirator. "I went over Bailey's homework with her and I read Hannah's favorite story, *Oh, The Places You'll Go*. You know, the Dr. Suess one?"

Nina nodded blankly. Of course she knew but was shocked that Derek still did.

"She still loves it," Derek added and turned back to the oven.

Nina put away the grocery items, wondering what had happened to her husband. It had been ages since he'd cooked. Even his occasionally putting the kids to bed on his own had been a long lost practice.

Derek clumsily moved around the kitchen, grabbing, chopping and wiping his hands in between.

"Do you want some help?" Nina offered.

"No, no, no," Derek rushed to shut the oven off. "No thanks, I got it." His eyes darted around, scanning the countertops, as he wiped his hands off on a kitchen towel. "At least I hope I do."

Nina's suspicion turned to fear as she added up the situation: Derek's above-and-beyond behavior, his accommodating attitude and this radical change. Nina's pulse quickened and her mouth got suddenly dry. She had to ask, and the words tumbled out.

"Derek, did you get fired today?"

He stopped chopping and looked up.

"What? No!" Derek shot back but quickly softened. "Look, I know this whole scenario probably seems a little, well weird. Like me showing up in a ... a cheetah-skin unitard and Viking helmet, right?" They both laughed. "But it didn't used to be. And no, I didn't get fired."

Nina cracked a relieved smile.

"I just wanted to have a night together and relax. I've been traveling and you've been hustling here, there and everywhere with the girls. I just thought it would be nice."

Derek did his best to recreate the meal Arnold had made for him. He had taken meticulous notes and even called Arnold before Nina got home for some last minute coaching. It was all starting to look the same as the meal he'd enjoyed so much. He hoped it would taste the same too. The "fruits of the earth" pudding would have been a bust, but Ruby, bless her heart, had some chokecherries in the freezer and sent them home with Derek.

He set the table, lit some candles and served a meal that was so good it astonished them both.

"Thank you for doing this, Derek. It's so nice," Nina said over a forkful of salad.

"I'm just happy it turned out okay," Derek mumbled between chews. "Oh, I'm headed to Arizona tomorrow."

"Phoenix?"

"No, Ft. Defiance. It's outside Window Rock," Derek added, trying in vain to clarify. "There's an Indian Health Service facility there and they have needs that ..." Derek saw Nina's crestfallen look and decided to tell her more. "I actually got offered my old territories back," Derek offered cautiously. "But I told Sedgewick I was happy where I was."

Nina looked at Derek like he'd sprouted a second head—or put on that unitard and helmet. "You ... turned him down?"

Derek nodded.

"But I thought that's what you wanted, Derek?" Nina asked softly.

"It was at first, but I think this change has been good for me. I'm going to smaller facilities, but the people are really nice. The places are quieter, lots of nature, less stress. It's given me time to think." Derek had almost said "run" but caught himself.

Nina listened and took a forkful of the buffalo schnitzel.

Derek saw that as a good sign and continued, "And I met some new friends too." Derek told Nina about the people he'd met, but especially Sarah, Arnold and Ruby. He'd said they'd not only been supportive friends, but also had been sharing their culture with Derek.

Nina nodded, knowing how important this was to him.

Derek had always said his background hadn't been that much of a concern to him, but she had always suspected otherwise. She had caught him on many occasions perusing the Native American section at bookstores and watching shows on Native history. Nina remembered the time they had gone to an art gallery and admired a painting of Jerome Tiger, a famous Creek artist, who painted a vibrantly colored scene of a Native village community. Derek had stared longingly, hypnotically at it as if in a trance.

Nina had been brought up to understand her roots and culture and sympathized that Derek hadn't been brought up in his. As Nina listened to Derek, she began to look past her own disappointment and see what working these rural territories meant to him. It wasn't another attempt to spin the situation. And it wasn't just what Derek was saying that moved Nina; it was how he was saying it. Nina could plainly see that Derek wanted this new state of things. He needed it. And she did too.

"I noticed you're wearing your wedding ring again." Nina cringed as soon as she said it. It sounded accusatory. But Derek seemed unfazed, as if he'd expected it.

"It didn't fit anymore," Derek said looking down at the gold band. "But now I've lost weight and it does. It wasn't that I didn't want to wear it, I just couldn't."

"You do look great," she said. Both of them blushed.

"I've lost quite a bit." Derek stood up and put his thumb in his waistband and pulled, making a large gap. "I guess Dr. Parker will be happy."

"I'm happy too, Derek. It's been the running, huh."

Derek's heart leapt. He wanted to tell Nina everything right then and there. "Yep. And I've been eating better too." Derek moved around the table, clearing plates. Nina got up to help him.

Derek said he'd do the dishes but Nina insisted on helping him with those as well. As the couple scrubbed and dipped the flatware and pots, Derek found himself feeling silly. He never imagined the act of washing dirty dishes together could be so sensual. But the candlelight, the warm, sudsy water and Nina's delicate hands tenderly touching his was intoxicating.

Derek and Nina retired to the couch and watched the last half of a cheesy sci-fi movie. Derek was oblivious to what played. He stared at his wife's beautiful profile in the glow of the illuminated screen. There was so much he wanted to tell her. It had been so long since they had snuggled closely like this and Nina seemed blissful, laughing at the movie and buried into Derek's side, holding his arm like a shield. Instead of spilling out, the words jammed in Derek's throat like chalky pills. He squeezed Nina tighter and buried his face in her soft and perfumed hair.

Days later, Derek was buffeted by wind and stung by the grit it carried. The rolling valley was sprinkled with green yucca plants and sagebrush on a background of red pepper dirt. The edges of the valley were lined with mesas and ochre sandstone giants. This was Navajo country, home of the Dine people. The smells of cooking meat wafted in the air. Mutton.

Derek burped up the flavor of that sheep he'd eaten today at an employee potluck at the clinic. Derek had a few potluck standards—baked beans and a deviled egg—but also had blue corn mush, squash blossoms and for the first time, mutton. These were traditional Navajo foods and Derek found the effects of eating mutton had been ... lasting.

"Geez, here we go again," Derek announced before he put his fist up to his lips to try and stop another gassy burp. "That sheep feels like it's trying to get back out." The jarring run and exertion hadn't helped his digestion.

Cole giggled.

A crow flew parallel to Derek for a moment and then darted off in a panic, unexpectedly seeing a giant sweaty creature at his flight level.

Derek told Cole about the meeting he'd had with Mr. Stone and what he'd learned as he watched the old curmudgeon—that the man's life was empty, regardless of financial wealth. But Cole seemed uninterested in Derek's breakthrough. Instead, he made comments about clouds, the birds and the landscape. Derek grew frustrated and quiet.

"Do you still love Mommy?" Cole finally broke the silence.

The question caught Derek off guard, slapping him with guilt. It seemed even Cole had noticed Derek's poor husbanding.

"Of course I do."

"She loves you, Daddy," Cole offered. "Mommy loves you very much."

"I know Cole."

"Bailey loves you very much too."

Derek frowned at the indictment. Now it seemed his poor fathering was being examined as well.

"I know she does Cole."

"And Hannah loves you very ..."

"Cole, I know that," Derek replied in a sing-song tone. "And that's a good thing."

"No, Daddy," Cole corrected. "It's the best thing!"

"Yeah?" Derek absently replied as he spied a dirt cloud rising on the far horizon behind a vehicle.

"Yes, Daddy. Life is love. It's the best thing there is—to give it and get it. The best thing," Cole said dreamily. "With love, we can endure anything. If we don't have it, we die because there's no reason to carry on."

Derek's eyes widened, following Cole's direction.

"Did that have something to do with why you died?"

"No, Daddy, that was different," Cole answered but didn't expand. "And Daddy ... He loves you too."

Derek understood who Cole spoke about but couldn't think of anything to say in reply. He wanted to believe this. He'd always wanted to. But to Derek the evidence proved otherwise.

How fortunate he was to have people around him that loved him. He was ashamed that he'd let his pride, his hurt, and his anger get in the way of giving and receiving love. The machinery of his heart seemed to stop running after Cole's death. Derek had been stuck in an emotional fog. Now that Cole had returned, the fog lifted and gears of his heart were loosening up and turning again. What Cole said made perfect sense. He'd been surrounded by love, propped up with it, and hadn't truly realized it until now. *Life was love.* What else was there, really? It was more important than his job, his pain, his pride. Without love, he had nothing and he knew it.

Derek thought of Mr. Stone again and how the man had more money than he could spend in ten lifetimes, yet was miserable. What good had it done him? What good had it done for others?

His parents never had much in the way of money. He remembered an image of a well-worn velveteen couch fraught with bald spots and an always-full pot of coffee. They had a frequent parade of visitors in their house that came to talk, share stories and bask in the kindness of the loving couple. His parents displayed so many traits that seemed to elude Derek. They measured their wealth in their relationships, the little joys—and in him. Derek flushed at the memory, humbled and embarrassed. He had put them through such hell at times and they loved him through it all.

"I wish I could tell your mom what was happening," Derek suggested, hoping Cole would agree.

"No, Daddy, you can't," Cole said. "But you could show her!"

Derek pondered that for a moment but his lungs ached and he knew he couldn't run much further. He wheezed and his throat burned from breathing in the hot vapors laced with dust. He could barely swallow the ropy strands of saliva. "I have to stop, Cole," Derek croaked. He slowed his pace and descended gently back down to the dirt trail, hearing Cole faintly.

"Bye bye, Daddy ..."

Derek was covered in crusty rings of red around the inside of his arms, his neck and the back of his legs from Martian dirt mixed with sweat. He finally recovered by the time he got back to the car in the parking lot of the local market. As he opened his door, a hand touched his arm. Derek turned to see a simply dressed Navajo man with a purple headband and his ashen hair tied in a neat bun. The old man was apparently with his grandson, a teenager with saggy jeans, a vacant expression and a t-shirt that read *Fry Bread Power.*

"He wants to give you something," the kid said as a matter of fact.

Derek was confused. The old man's eyes blazed as he spoke to Derek quietly in powerful, measured tones in the Navajo language. The old man seemed to be trying in earnest to communicate something to him with no success. The grandson was distracted during this, waving to friends on the other side of the parking lot. The elder pointed with his lips and turned to walk to his truck with Derek in tow. The grandson trotted to catch up. The old man dug through the glove box as the bored teen looked down and pushed buttons on his iPod. Derek awkwardly stood there, covered in grime and sweat, waiting for who knows what. The old man turned and offered a small leather pouch from his shaky hand.

"It's corn pollen," the grandson said casually.

"What's it for?" Derek asked.

"To pray with," the kid answered as he helped his grandfather into the truck.

Derek eyed the bag in his hand and asked, "Why's he giving it to me?"

The kid shrugged his shoulders and shut his grandfather's door for him. "Don't know, man," The young man answered as he pulled up his sagging pants so he could climb into the driver's seat. "He just said he needed to."

Derek stood in the parking lot as the faded green rattletrap truck reluctantly started then struggled away.

Over a bowl of chicken noodle soup, Derek examined the bag of corn pollen. He peeked into the bag at the brilliant yellow dust, as if looking at it would reveal some answers. Derek pulled the drawstring closed and stuffed it into his pocket. He sipped the wonderful soup and knew someone had made it with love. *That word again.* Derek reflected on Cole's words and on this key ingredient in the recipe of life. He knew he hadn't been making his contribution in love. The other ingredients were there—love from all around him and especially Nina and the girls—but the flavor of his life had soured and he realized it was his doing.

Cole even mentioned what Derek had always wanted to believe—that God did love him. But where had God been when Derek needed him most? Where had God been through all his struggles, his torments, his losses? To Derek, God had never favored him. But hadn't God sent Cole back to him? Was this not a loving act? Derek feared perhaps he was being set up for another heartbreak but couldn't see how that would develop. He didn't want to.

Derek grabbed his cell phone and punched in the numbers. After a few rings, the voice he wanted so badly to hear danced in his ears.

"Hello?" Nina answered, her warm voice almost drowned out by the girls singing loudly in the background.

"Hi Nina. It's me." Derek realized he sounded dramatic.

"Are you okay?" Nina asked, suddenly serious and hushing the girls.

"Oh, yeah, I'm fine. I just called to …" Derek stopped short of saying the sappy cliché in an 80's hit by Stevie Wonder. The words welled up inside of him. He pictured Nina's face in his mind and the delicate freckles scattered across her nose and cheeks like cinnamon sprinkles and said it anyway. "... to say I love you."

The phone was silent and Derek held his breath.

"I love you too, Derek," Nina said tenderly. "Are you sure everything is okay?"

Derek breathed relief.

"I'm sure. I just wanted to tell you that." Derek felt lighter somehow and not so alone. Such simple words but they'd seemed to redeem. "And tell the girls I love them too, okay?"

"I will, Derek."

Skip looked down and reread the e-mail for the fifth time. He couldn't believe it. His emotions were in a mental blender and wondered how this would affect his days ahead at Global Medix. Would he be next? He stood up from his chair and paced around the office, deliberating what to do. What he could do? The room seemed to shrink in around him and the racket of the copier down the hall was more annoying than usual.

He knew he had to connect with Derek as soon as possible. His trembling hand tried to dial the numbers three times before he got it right. The phone went to voicemail but Skip knew it wouldn't be appropriate to leave a message about this. He mumbled angrily to no one in particular and started texting.

Meanwhile, Derek imagined he was on a bad carnival ride. The small plane ran a gauntlet through the clouds, slapped and punched by wind and rain. He tightened his seatbelt and took a sip of water from his bottle. He thought of Buddy Holly, the Big Bopper and Richie Valens. Wasn't this the way they met their end? Small plane. Bad weather.

Derek shook his head to throw the thoughts out of his brain. He wished he was home. He wished Cole was talking with him. He looked around and saw a handful of other passengers in their own private worlds of concern.

A gaunt man with a shock of gray hair and a loose tie snored loudly with his mouth hanging open. The stack of papers in his hands was dangerously close to spilling on the floor. Derek wondered if he would end up like this—exhausted enough to sleep through violent turbulence. He pictured an older version of himself, traveling endlessly like a lost soul, trying to make his sales numbers each month for products that failed to stir his passion. He returned to the thoughts of the day the music died. It seemed less miserable.

Just when it seemed certain the plane would tear itself apart, the craft popped out of a charcoal fog into the sunlight and calm air. The passengers in the cabin emitted a collective gasp of relief. The snoring man went on sleeping. Derek pressed his face to the window and saw giant piles of cotton candy clouds, illuminated pink by the setting sun and outlined in bright purple. The orange sherbet sun melted into the far horizon. The plane floated peacefully over the colorful blanket and Derek trembled. He didn't know why but simply smiled and took in the beauty. He was grateful to be in the moment, and for the first time in a long time, he prayed. Derek didn't pray for anything. He prayed a simple prayer of thanks—for everything.

The plane landed with a violent thump and lurched forward. The sleeping man finally woke just in time for his papers to shoot down the aisle when the pilot applied the brakes. Derek turned on his cell as the plane bumped its way to the terminal. He saw that he'd received a text from Skip and opened it up. It read *Big changes going on at work. Call me as soon as you land.*

Derek called and Skip answered after the first ring.

"Derek, I'm glad you called."

"What's up?"

Skip's voice wavered. "Global Medix will be going through a reorganization. A big one." Derek knew the corporate euphemism meant people would be losing their jobs. His blood ran cold. He knew his company had been going through some recent challenges but had no idea it would come to this.

"And?" Derek struggled to ask.

"And it looks like you and I are going to be separated, buddy."

Derek considered this a weird way to be told he'd lost his job. "You mean I'm …"

"I mean we're both getting new bosses in different departments," Skip continued.

Derek was now completely lost.

"What's going on, Skip? How did that happen?"

"It's Sedgewick. He's being laid off."

CHAPTER 10

THE NEXT DAY, Derek lingered in the Global Medix break room after pouring a cup of coffee. A gloom hung over the entire facility since news of the layoffs broke. People were quiet. People were scared. In this solitary snack room, the bright colors of the vending machines and a few posters with pictures of nature and goofy motivational sayings provided a refuge. He stirred the cream into his coffee ever so slowly, delaying the inevitable. Derek almost dumped his cup when Skip poked his head in the doorway.

"Whoa, easy buddy," Skip said.

Derek tossed his stirrer into the trash and asked, "How's he doing?"

"I don't know. He's been pretty quiet today, kind of like a zombie." Skip looked down. "I think he's in shock."

"He's not the only one," Derek said.

"There was another thing I found out. He went to bat for both of us, and that's why we still have jobs."

Skip hadn't needed the backing to keep his job, but Derek knew he surely did. He felt worse than before.

"Well, I've got to go meet up with my new boss, Roger Simon," Skip said. "I heard he's a good guy."

"I heard that too," Derek nodded. "I'll be up on the fifth floor, so ..."

"Remember, no matter what happens, I will find you," Skip said, parroting the cheesy line from the movie *Last of the Mohicans*. Since Derek was the only Native American employee at their company, it fit perfectly and Skip scored another winning jest. Plus, he said it with the same passion Daniel Day-Lewis had when he delivered the line to his love interest in the movie. The two laughed out loud. It helped.

Derek walked down the hall feeling the gravity in every step. He came to the open door and saw his former boss packing his possessions into the cardboard boxes, looking fondly for a moment at a framed family picture in his hand. There were times when Derek thought he truly hated this man, but his heart was breaking for him now. Even Sedgewick's toupee seemed dull and lifeless today. Derek knew the man was a loose cannon at times, but overall a decent man. Sedgewick did his best to take care of his people and business, usually in that order.

Derek found out the reorganization had been done to boost stock prices by less than one half of one percent. Pathetic. No one could ever argue that Sedgewick hadn't worked tirelessly for the benefit of this company, made great sacrifices, and yet when times got tough, they chose to dump him for a microscopic boost in stock prices that probably wouldn't last to the weekend.

The irony wasn't lost on Derek. He realized it should have been him that was canned. At times he secretly wished for that. But here stood Sedgewick, the go-getter, the coach of the team and the ever-faithful cheerleader, boxing up his things to join the exodus from Global Medix. Sedgewick looked up at Derek and sadly smiled.

"Come in, Derek. I was hoping you'd stop by before I left."

Derek felt guilty he hadn't come sooner.

"I wanted to say something to you, son." Sedgewick looked uncomfortable but said it anyway. "I'm sorry."

Derek was taken aback. "What on earth for? You saved my job," he admitted. "More than once."

Sedgewick shook his head and continued. "But I took you off the front line and onto the rural clients."

Derek couldn't let Sedgewick leave his job thinking he'd screwed him over. Without the territory change, Derek wouldn't have had the time to reflect, to run and to connect with Cole. He wouldn't have met Arnold, Ruby or Sarah. Sedgewick had done him no wrong and in fact, he had done him a favor.

"No, sir, I didn't see it that way at all." Derek realized his statement seemed unbelievable. "I mean, I did at first, but I deserved it."

Sedgewick opened his mouth to speak, but Derek waved his hand and continued.

"No, I did, I know. But I like my new clients and my new schedule. That's why I turned down the offer to get my bigger clients back. This has been good for me in more ways than you could imagine."

Sedgewick softened, appreciating the words. He looked around the office and seemed forlorn but still smiled.

"I'm going to miss this place."

Derek looked down at the boxes, not knowing what to say.

"But, hey, this gives me more time with the grandkids and golf, right?"

Derek nodded.

"Keep up the good work, Derek. I'm proud of you, son." Sedgewick hit Derek's shoulder in his usual manner, too hard, and went back to his task.

When Derek returned home that night, he walked through the door and into the kitchen. Nina was on the phone while she cooked and Hannah and Bailey were diligently making a craft with Popsicle sticks and paint. The place was a royal mess, but Derek was happy to be home. He placed a kiss on the back of Nina's neck. She scrunched her shoulder and spun around, beaming with delight. Derek went to his girls, lost in their activity and squeezed them together, kissing them on the tops of their heads in turn. Joy surged though him not because he still had a job, but because he still had his family.

"Mom says hi," Nina said. "And Dr. Parker's office called back to schedule your annual physical."

Derek hadn't had an annual physical in years and then realized Dr. Parker had clever ways to get patients to come back in for follow ups. Actually, Derek looked forward to going, sure that he'd impress the doctor with his weight loss and maybe lower blood pressure and a cholesterol level too. Between the running and his improved diet, Derek had to buy a couple new shirts and pairs of pants.

"I'll call tomorrow and set it up," Derek said.

"I already did," Nina replied. "I know he's going to be very impressed."

The family sat around the table for dinner. Nina made grilled tilapia, wild rice and steamed veggies. Derek spied her several times, watching him as he interacted with the kids. Derek looked up laughing after Bailey told a joke and caught Nina staring at him. The two locked eyes and Derek could feel love glowing inside of him. It was good to be home.

The next morning Derek flew to South Dakota for another business trip. After the day's meetings, he drove to Arnold and Ruby's home.

"Hau Kola," Arnold opened the door to Derek.

"Hau to you too Kola," Derek replied and caught the sweet, smoky smell of burning wood. He always felt goofy adding English into the Lakota phrases but just couldn't seem to help himself. Arnold just always chuckled.

Several days earlier Derek had asked Arnold about conducting another sweatlodge and Arnold had readily agreed. The two shook hands and walked through the house. Arnold flicked off an old episode of *F Troop* as they walked by the TV.

After they changed into shorts and flip-flops, the two walked out the back door into the backyard. The stones were already shimmering red in the dying fire.

"Derek, can I ask you something?" Arnold asked as he arranged some ceremonial items on the small dirt mound that served as an altar outside the lodge.

"Sure," Derek said, though he suddenly grew nervous.

"Have you lost someone—I mean, recently?"

Derek knew it would do no good to lie and didn't want to anyway. His throat tightened, so he simply nodded.

"You know, in our traditions, we mourn the loss of loved ones for one year and no more." Arnold gingerly placed his prayer pipe on the altar. "The time is limited for a reason because life must go on."

Derek nodded again and realized it had indeed been a full year since Cole's death.

"I could tell you've been carrying a heavy burden since we met," Arnold said. "I'm glad you wanted to come back to sweat again."

"And there's something I've been meaning to ask you," Derek said. "What the heck does toka hoka … hok,"

"Toka hokshila," Arnold answered. "It basically means 'young man of a different tribe'."

Derek inwardly smiled after being referred to as belonging to a tribe, any tribe. His memories of being Indian had always been negative and involved slurs against him. Arnold's words were ointment to those wounds.

"This sweat will be a little different. I'll try to work on you to remove that pain but it's up to the spirits," Arnold said. He grabbed some hot coals out of the fire with a shovel and dropped them into an old coffee can with a makeshift wire handle. He then tore at some branches of flat cedar and dropped the bits into the can. The thick perfume of the smoke washed over them both and the foliage sizzled and popped. Next, Arnold grabbed a large fan made of eagle feathers on an intricately beaded handle.

To Derek, the dark gray fan with a slight sheen reminded him of an enormous seal flipper.

Arnold said prayers and used the fan to waft the smoke onto Derek as he held the can in front of him.

"Medicine," Arnold said and they both nodded.

Derek could feel a familiar buzz growing within him as Arnold prayed over him. Suddenly, a fear filled him and he wondered if this ceremony would sever the connection to Cole. Arnold walked around Derek, praying and fanning. Derek's fear turned to panic as the buzzing grew. On the verge of demanding a stop to the ceremony, he opened his eyes and saw Arnold staring at him with his mouth agape and a rattled expression. He had stopped fanning.

"What's wrong?" Derek asked.

"Nothing," Arnold quickly answered. "Let's go in, huh?"

The two made preparations to sweat, saying the prayers, loading the pipe. Arnold crawled in as Derek clumsily carried hot rocks from the fire on the tines of a pitchfork. Arnold gently moved the grandfathers into place with his deer antler and looked into the glowing red orbs for guidance. When all the rocks had been carried in, Derek appeared at the doorway on his hands and knees, like an eager kid ready to enter a tent on his first camping trip.

The songs and smoke carried their prayers into the night. Derek was getting familiar with the songs and joined in with spotty success. When the two emerged after the sweat, a wave of thick white steam exited the lodge with them. The flushed men glistened as they stood between the fire and the moonlight in the cool air. Hazy vapors rose from their bodies like ghosts.

Derek felt rejuvenated, purified. And lighter somehow. He couldn't put a finger on the source of it, but Arnold had told him before that it's not important to verbalize the feelings, just to feel blessed for having them.

As the two smoked the pipe together, Arnold prayed for guidance. Conflict concerning what he'd seen in Derek clawed at him. He debated whether he should tell him or not and elected to wait until Tunkashila, the Creator, gave him more insight into what it meant. Arnold had faith that the explanation and meaning would come in time. For now, all he had was the vision: a very bright and powerful light that surrounded Derek and that seemed warm and loving. But there was also something else, a darkness inside of Derek—an ominous, charcoal-colored blob with long, slender tentacles wrapping around Derek's insides. The force seemed determined not to release its grip on Derek. Both the radiant light and the dull object seemed to be alive and existing in balance, neither making a move toward the other. Arnold worried about the vision. He had seen that dull blackness once before in a healing ceremony he did for a cousin many years ago. Two months later that cousin was dead.

Arnold and Derek said their goodbyes. Derek seemed cheerful, which made Arnold's burden heavier. As Derek drove off into the night, Arnold went back inside to grab his pipe and then went back outside down to the fire. He pinched some tobacco from his pouch and held it up to the stars. Fear tangled his mind and spirit. He pleaded in his mumbled prayers with that pinch thrust forward, his eyes tightly closed. A tear filled the trench of his scar down the side of his face.

The next morning, Derek rose from his squeaky bed and stretched his arms skyward, uttering weird noises that made him laugh. He was headed home today after hitting a few clinics in the area in as many days. He had placed several orders and continued to be captivated by the hospitality of his new clientele. The facilities were sparse, the resources scarce, but the dedication and commitment of the Indian Health Service providers he met truly inspired him. He sat down at his rickety coffee table and entered the order details on his laptop.

Derek checked the clock and saw he had several hours before the flight. *Time for a run.* He splashed water on his face, got dressed and wandered next door to get a coffee.

"What can I getcha, dear?" asked the gum-chewing waitress with a beehive hairdo.

"Just coffee, please." Derek scanned the quiet patrons eating sausage and gravy, bacon and grease-covered eggs. None of it even seemed tempting anymore. All those things would only serve to slow him down and he couldn't allow that to happen.

"Hey, you're that guy from a couple months ago from, uh," the waitress flicked her pencil against her head dangerously close to her eye. "San Diego?"

Derek nodded.

"My, honey, you've lost some weight. You been sick or somethin'?"

"Nope, just working out," Derek said, patting his belly.

"We've got a special today that's fit for a king."

"Just coffee, thanks." Derek glanced at his watch. He wanted to get going.

Derek noticed the mornings were much cooler now and a few leaves were turning color. Change was coming. Derek's Achilles tendon had been stiff for the last couple weeks but as always, after a few minutes, it loosened. He quickly found his stride even before the buzzing started. Electricity filled his veins, gentle pressure enveloped his body, and his shoes lifted off the crunching gravel.

"Good morning, son. It's a beautiful day, isn't it?"

"Sure is, Daddy!"

Derek shot up ten feet higher after hearing the boy's voice. He thought about the paradox of feeling angry at God for so much but grateful for this connection to Cole. The two talked about the shapes of the clouds and birds dancing on the wind. Derek finally had to ask.

"If God loves me so much, why has he done things to cause pain my whole life? Was sending you back an attempt to make that all better?"

"No, Daddy, it wasn't. Your life has already been filled with good and if you didn't have the hurts, you'd never know it."

Derek's silence exposed his confusion.

"What did you do when I died?" Cole asked.

The question upset Derek but he answered, "I cried. I cried because we lost you."

"Then what did you do?"

Derek was back in that moment of suffering, reviewing his actions.

"I don't know," he answered.

"What did you do in the hallway outside of the NICU?" Cole asked.

The flash of the image and emotion filled Derek's mind. "I hugged your mom and sisters with all my might," he said. "I cried with them and told them over and over I loved them."

Derek clearly remembered the desperation of that moment. Life had crumbled around him and he clung to the ones he loved like never before. In that moment, he had been … grateful for those he had in his life. But in time, Derek's attitude changed. He grew bitter and his bitterness turned to hatred. And then to apathy.

Derek believed his life had been filled with fear, pain, loss and anger. He had become spiteful toward God, thinking the entity a cheat and a thief. He had become adept at attributing his hard luck, his lot and his disappointments as another vengeful act from a vengeful God. He kept a running count of the losses and the beatings and had determined to hold the grudge of the anger forever. He blamed God for his own poor decisions and choices. God became an emotional punching bag, a lightning rod of blame, that Derek had been for so long as a child. Convinced God had it out for him, he returned the favor with vicious conviction.

But Derek now realized that he'd missed out on other things that were painted onto the canvas of his life. He'd looked at these things all his life yet never really saw them. He'd never thanked God once for the Sorensens taking him in and saving him from the hell of the abusive families he'd been with. He never acknowledged a true sense of gratitude for Nina or the birth of his girls, instead feeling it was the least God could do to mend past transgressions. Of course, he loved them all, but he realized he was never thankful for them all.

Images of Skip, Arnold, Ruby and even Sedgewick, the man who had saved Derek's job, entered his mind. Had these people not been a blessing to him when he needed one most? He had never been thankful for the opportunities he'd had in school or the kind teachers that encouraged him. He thought of his health, his home, his life and the countless good things that rushed by in a flood of images. He suddenly felt very petty. He had taken twisted satisfaction from dumping the bad at God's feet, but had never once thanked him for the joys and blessings he'd been given. Derek saw his life as he never had before. He saw that his *life was good.*

Derek saw Cole's words made perfect sense. Life was pain but it was also joy. We need both elements or neither would make sense or have any meaning. He recalled of one of his favorite poets, Rod McKuen, who said in poem *Eight:*

> *"You have to make the good times yourself*
> *take the little times and make them into big times*
> *and save the times that are all right*
> *for the ones that aren't so good"*

Derek had read that years ago, many times, but the words didn't register until this moment. He took comfort, not in the fact that the bad would go away, but that the good would always be there with it and it was up to him to look for it. And to be grateful when he found it.

Derek tilted his head forward and the view hit him like a hammer. He was higher than he'd ever been before, soaring over the sweeping prairie like an eagle. He was hundreds of feet high and climbing.

"Weeeee!" Cole exclaimed.

Derek joined in with a yell of his own. He felt transformed and exuberant, like seeing the sun for the first time. And for the first time in his life, he felt free.

Derek laughed loudly and suddenly started to gurgle and gag. Cole giggled like a pot boiling over. Derek violently shook his head and closed his eyes. Cole laughed even harder.

Finally Derek caught his breath and grinned, exposing jagged black splotches and tiny wings in the cracks of his teeth. "Nothing like bugs for breakfast!"

Back in San Diego the next day, Derek sat on the exam table, swinging his legs and grinning like a kid on Christmas. He had made good on his word and finally came in last week for a physical with Dr. Parker. As he expected, Dr. Parker was thoroughly impressed with Derek's transformation. Derek's weight was way down and so was his blood pressure. Dr. Parker had done a full work up on Derek and sent him to the lab to get blood drawn, conducting a complete blood count and panel to check cholesterol and other vital stats.

Derek's only complaint had been a nagging, persistent jaw pain that resulted from one of the more spectacular crash landings he had over a month ago. Of course, Derek said it had been caused by an accident with a car door opening. Dr. Parker sent him to X-ray just to be sure there was no fracture. Derek waited impatiently at this follow up for Dr. Parker to deliver what was sure to be marked improvement in his cholesterol.

When Dr. Parker walked in with the X-rays, Derek had forgotten he'd had them done since the jaw pain had all but disappeared. Dr. Parker's drawn face and the stranger with him piqued Derek's curiosity.

"Derek, this is Dr. Banfield. He's our Chief of Oncology," Dr. Parker said as he inserted X-ray prints into the lighted panels.

Derek shook the man's hand, confused.

"Well, how'd my blood work go?" Derek's confusion blossomed into fear.

"Your cholesterol is way down and several other factors looked much improved. I'm sure because of the running." Dr. Parker pushed his glasses back up on his nose. "And your jaw's fine. But there were other things that made me suspicious when I looked at the X-rays, so I consulted with Dr. Banfield."

Derek looked at the films of his head and noticed some white balls within the border of his skull. He looked up at Dr. Parker, but the doctor looked away. Derek remembered Dr. Parker saying how he absolutely hated being friends with his patients when he had devastating news. But it was Dr. Banfield that finally spoke.

For Derek, the next several minutes were surreal, like watching a movie starring someone else. His mouth went slack and he stared at the doctor's Danish clogs as he heard terms like *stage three*, *inoperable* and *not much time*. But the words that rang loudest were the first spoken and they had unraveled Derek's mind and took the very breath from his lungs.

Derek, you've got cancer.

CHAPTER 11

DEREK REFUSED THE offer to be driven home or to have someone called to pick him up from the hospital. Both Dr. Parker's and Dr. Banfield's voices had become like Charlie Brown's teacher repeated endlessly in Derek's mind. He walked out of the clinic and tried to process what happened but the whole interaction had left him dazed. The doctors wanted to run more tests and discussed palliative care options since the disease was advanced. They had discussed probable symptoms like nausea, dizziness and general weakness. To his doctor's surprise, and his, Derek hadn't had any of these yet. But the final symptom mentioned bothered him. Dr. Banfield said that patients with such advanced brain cancer can experience vivid and realistic hallucinations.

The drive home was a blur and Derek walked into the house, feeling now more than ever, like a temporary visitor in his own home ... in his own life. He reflected on how this seemed reminiscent of his foster home days, biding his time until a new home was found. But Derek didn't want to leave. He desperately wanted to stay and hadn't realized how much until now.

Nina and girls were out on errands so the house stood frozen in stillness. Derek could hear his own breath in the lonely front room and a shudder ran through his body. Responding as he had much of his life, the fear turned quickly to anger.

He changed his clothes and drove to an isolated stretch of beach as the sun went down. Had this whole connection to Cole been a wishful dream? Had the flying simply been a fantasy created by a brain fighting an illness? Derek needed to find out. He jumped out of the car and dashed across the parking lot onto the sand, forgoing a stretch or warm up. The thick, salted air blew in stiffly from the ocean and smelled of decaying seaweed. With no ramp up of his tempo, Derek sprinted, desperate to connect as soon as he could. The buzzing wasn't pleasant or gentle as it had been but hit him like a static discharge throughout his body, jolting him off the sand a few feet.

"Cole!" Derek demanded.

"Yes, Daddy," the voice came back serene and expectant.

"You knew, didn't you!" Derek barked.

"Yes."

"You knew and you didn't tell me I was dying of cancer?"

"Mmmm hmmm," Cole answered softly.

"But why, Cole?" Derek pleaded, choking on his words.

"Everyone dies in time and it's usually better not to know when until you have to."

His chest heaved and the words provided no salve to his rage. He was betrayed. God, the ultimate thief, had played his final hand and would leave him with nothing in the end. He could feel bile building in the back of his throat, unsure if it was because of this realization or the intense pace. He was already soaked in sweat and gasping. Was this the first sign that he was indeed sick and dying?

Derek slowed to an uncoordinated jog, stumbled and finally fell onto his hands and knees with his hands disappearing under the cool, ashen sand. He saw the beginning of the end, hands already buried. The rest of him would follow soon. He dry heaved over the sand.

"You win, God!" Derek leaned back on his knees and screamed skyward. "You are God and I am nothing! You win, you miserable ..." He started choking and dry heaving again. "I knew it. I knew it all along ... you win." He no longer felt anger. He didn't feel fear. He realized he didn't feel anything anymore and surrendered.

Derek got up and walked back to the car, mumbling obscenities and caustic surrenders until he finally walked in silence. Apathy now ruled him and he saw his life as a lost cause, a sad tale of a man God had damned in this world before he ever had a chance. *Didn't God do this to someone in the Bible? Joshua or Job? They got screwed too. God was no rescuer of people. He was the cruelest of kings.*

He felt betrayed by Cole as well but couldn't bring himself to feel anger over it. There would be no more bargaining, no more actions to be taken except to get his life in order for Nina and the girls. He maneuvered his slack body into the car and turned on the engine. He headed home but felt lost.

When he arrived, Hannah and Bailey were already fast asleep. Derek kept Nina at a distance and gave a censored version of his doctor's visit, electing not to tell her anything tonight. He was spent. And she'd know the truth soon enough.

He closed his eyes, exhausted to his core, and the warm, sinking sensation of sleep took hold of him. Suddenly his eyes flew open. He was driving down an icy highway and moonlight bathed the snow banks on the side of the road. *How did I get here?* Derek could feel the tires breaking loose in the turn. The car weaved wildly to the left and right of the double yellow lines. He was going too fast but he couldn't stop.

In a spray of snow lit by the halogen headlights, Derek's car slammed into a boulder on the side of the road with a sickening crunch and the scream of tortured metal, snapping plastic and shattering glass. And then complete quiet.

Derek felt snowflakes gently falling on his face. Though dazed, he was regaining awareness and realized he'd had an accident. The bitter cold was everywhere at once and silence, save a rhythmic hiss as something hot dripped onto something cold. *How the hell did I get here? Where am I?* He watched snow falling through the beam of one headlight as a warm wetness ran down his face.

The smell of gas jolted Derek to action and he tried to move. He quickly realized he was stuck in the seatbelt, the twisted metal and the steering wheel crushing in on his chest. He furrowed his brow in disappointment, knowing he'd surely miss the sales meeting now. He imagined of the hassle of insurance and the grief the rental car company would give him for totaling their car. He snickered, realizing the absurdity of those thoughts given his immediate bind.

Suddenly Derek sensed the gravity of his predicament. Anger turned to fear and fear turned to panic. He struggled to reach his cell phone. It was dead.

Captive in the broken car, Derek's mind wandered to his family. He saw Nina combing Hannah's hair as Bailey did her homework. Ashamed, he revisited his last interactions with them all. Nina had told Derek, "I love you" and gently kissed his cheek. Derek had feigned sleep and didn't respond. He'd yelled at Hannah for bothering him while he was reading the paper. And he had hardly spoken to Bailey in nearly a week—had it been that long? More than his injuries, he suffered guilt and regret. These hurts cut deeper.

Derek released choking sobs into the starry skies. He began to beg, first in his mind, then aloud, for his life. He pleaded for one more day of this precious and dying gift. *Why is this happening to me?* After several minutes, Derek became woozy and drained. He had watched enough late night medical shows in his hotel room to know what was happening. He looked at the steaming pool collecting near the floor mat and knew it was coming from him. The blood looked like liquid ebony in the dim light of the moon. Outside the car a puddle of oil grew. Man and machine were both dying.

Derek's breath grew shallow and he felt cold. The pain was fading along with his heartbeat. He held the image of his wife and children in his mind and saw them as if for the first time. *Please, I can't leave now.* What a beautiful family he had. *Just a few more days, God. A few hours. Anything, please.* He would miss them so. He prayed as images from his life randomly flashed in his mind.

In the distance he heard the faint whine of a siren but knew it was too late. He was losing everything he had or would ever hope to have. The siren grew louder and more familiar. He could barely see the soft pulse of red lights on the snow and then everything was gone.

Derek opened his eyes. He saw the flashing red light of the digital display reading 6:25 a.m. and heard the rhythmic cry of the alarm. Nina rolled over, moaning, and fumbled for her glasses. She sat up with unkempt hair and lazily smiled.

"I'll get the coffee," she mumbled.

Derek couldn't say a word as she flicked on the TV and walked out of the bedroom. He quickly touched his face, his body, checking for wounds. The dream was more vivid than he'd ever dreamed before. Was it a hallucination from the brain tumor? Did it matter? His whole body shuddered with the relief that comes in such moments. He was alive.

"Life's a beautiful gift," the smiling preacher proclaimed on the television. It seemed a lifetime ago that Derek had first heard this in his motel room, but the dream he'd just had confirmed it.

"You got that right, my man," Derek replied. He lay in bed and wept. He now believed the whispered voice he'd been hearing wasn't Cole's; it had been his. *Life is now, life is love, life is good.* This was going to be a good day. And so would tomorrow. And the next one after that, through the remainder of the precious time he had left. He would see to it. He jumped up and ran to scoop the kids from their beds.

Derek sat at the breakfast bar without eating. He didn't even have coffee. He simply marveled in wonder as Hannah and Bailey ate their cereal. Nina poured a cup of coffee and sipped it, watching Derek. He looked at Nina, nodding his head toward the girls, as if to say, "Get a load of these two."

Nina got the girls ready for school and Derek helped them pick clothes and load their backpacks, making silly faces at them the whole time.

"Don't you have to go to work today?" Nina finally asked.

"Yeah, I guess," Derek said absently as he tied Hannah's shoe as she giggled.

"I guess?" Nina retorted.

"Well, I'll call in and let them know I'll be late."

Before Nina could question him, Derek bounded downstairs with the girls to load them into the minivan. Nina drove and Derek sat with the window down and his face turned to the sun, eyes closed as if dreaming. They dropped the girls off at school and Derek hugged Hannah and Bailey like a child hugs their favorite doll, with endless love. Nina wondered if Derek had gotten a promotion or closed a record-breaking sale.

When they got home, Derek said nothing of his news but shut the door and pulled Nina close to him. Almost nose to nose, Nina's warm breath danced on his lips, and he put his mouth onto hers. After a long, deep kiss, he pulled back and beheld her as if he hadn't seen her in years.

"I love you, Nina," Derek said. "I always have and I'm so sorry I haven't shown you more, that I haven't told you more."

Nina glowed.

"You've made my life what it is—good beyond words—and I want you to know that. Without you, my life would be an empty place."

Derek reached for her hand and led her upstairs. It had been so long since they'd made love, but the wait had only intensified the act, making their love new again.

The two lay in bed, gazing at the ceiling.

"Did you ever call in to work?" Nina suddenly asked.

"No, I forgot," Derek said.

Nina sat up in bed, her wild hair cascading down her front like a beautiful, disheveled mermaid. "What's going on, Derek?"

Her question tore Derek from his reverie. He had been enjoying this moment and wanted to stay there, but he knew it was time to come clean.

He sat up in bed and his hair looked like it had been done with an egg beater. Nina smiled at the sight.

"I've got cancer," Derek said.

Nina's smile froze to her face. "You've got what?"

The painful conversation that followed was one all too familiar to Nina. The words her mom had used to describe her father's cancer were oddly similar to the words Derek was using to describe his. Her mom had laced the news with warm niceties and gentle tones, as Derek did now. Nina didn't cry because she refused to believe this was an insurmountable challenge. This was not the end, only the beginning of research, treatment options and get well plans. With shaking hands, she fumbled on the nightstand for her cell phone to look up numbers to call.

Derek pushed a lock of hair away from her eyes then took her hands in his. He said softly, "It's okay, Nina."

She bit her lip and trembled.

"It's okay, honey," Derek repeated.

Nina jerked her hands away and jolted out of bed, her naked figure radiant in the sunlight, covered in glowing stripes from the slatted blinds.

"No, it's not okay! We need to get a second opinion. We need to figure this out." Nina was almost yelling.

The fire in Nina's eyes showed the determination that she would fight for his life even if the doctors believed it was too late already. Derek agreed that he pursue second opinions and be open to any treatment options they could find. Nina frantically punched numbers into the cellphone. He got out of bed and walked over to her. He kissed her forehead and then got dressed. He had things to do too.

In the days that followed, Derek turned to the morbid yet mundane tasks at hand in the form of paperwork that would get make his life's exit survivable, and hopefully even comfortable, for Nina and the girls. Luckily they already had a will, a modest portfolio and college funds set up for Hannah and Bailey. He considered the countless details he hadn't expected to have to think about for many years to come. He took notes on the only pad of paper he could find: Bailey's *American Girl* notebook. He wrote quickly, surprised at feeling a lack of fear or anger, not because he was detached, but because he was deeply engaged in his life and this moment. He aimed to get these things squared away as soon as possible so he could enjoy the time he had left with his family.

As he pinpointed the details he'd need to address in the weeks to come, he appraised other things that he needed to resolve in his life, beyond paperwork and legal documents.

He could hear Nina talking excitedly on the phone and running back and forth down the hall. He felt sorry for her, realizing what she was going through. He wished he could spare Nina this pain. His heart descended further when he contemplated how they would tell the girls and when.

True to his word, Derek went back for more tests with Dr. Banfield and his team. They did blood work, MRIs, cat scans and used every piece of equipment Derek had ever sold. It seemed every opening on his body was probed and where there wasn't a hole, the doctors created one. The astronauts in the space program couldn't have gone through so much medical testing.

Regardless of the test, the answers kept coming back the same. Derek had multiple late-stage, inoperable tumors in his brain. Steering clear of announcing the death sentence details, the doctors said Derek had three to six months of "good health" left. The series of tests ended with discussions of palliative care, radiation and possible new medications not designed to stop the tumors but to mitigate the symptoms for as long as possible.

After several whirlwind weeks, Derek and Nina decided they'd heard enough and accepted the news. Derek had already been on medical leave from Global Medix, but the two agreed it was time for full disclosure on the situation. They drove back from their new second home, the hospital, and the quiet was stifling. The hollowed out look in Nina's eyes told Derek she was operating on auto-pilot.

"Please don't look at this as a defeat," Derek said.

"How can you say that?" Nina asked. She stared out the passenger window with puffy eyes. "Really, Derek. How can you say that?" She turned her head to him, daring him to answer.

"Because we all die sometime, Nina." Derek gripped the wheel tighter. "But it's what we do with the time we have that really matters, right? To love others and be loved back, that's the best we can hope for in this life." Derek reached one hand out to her. "And we have that, Nina."

Nina gripped his hand tightly and sobbed as she nodded.

Derek had agreed to take what the doctors hoped would be next new wonder drug, the experimental Promaxonex, though they cautioned there may be side effects as listed in the mighty stack of paperwork they'd received that day. It was Nina's idea and Derek didn't argue, knowing it gave her some sense of control of an uncontrollable state.

Derek's seemingly quick acceptance of his situation was judged by many around him as shock or delusional thinking and drew pity. He accepted it, knowing everyone coped in their own way.

He happily helped as much as possible with the kids and savored the moments like bites of a fine French meal. Daily interactions took on a new light and color for Derek. He talked to Nina about visiting his parents to deliver the news in person, not over the phone. Nina offered to go with him, the girls too if he wanted, but he gently declined, determined to make this a solo visit. Besides, he had some other things to get settled back home.

Derek landed in Oklahoma City on a beautiful fall day. It was warm, the humidity was low, and the leaves were a rainbow of changing colors. He was humbled to realize that even though he appreciated things in his life more than ever, it didn't stop him from being upset with the rude guy in the rental car line. The jerk in the plaid sport coat spoke at full volume on his cell phone, smelling like there had been an epic battle between his rank body odor and the cheap cologne he'd tried to cover it with. There were no winners.

Derek caught himself frequently looking at his watch, as if counting the hours down. How many hours were in a week or month? Or in three to six months? He'd have to check on that. Seeing the leaves change was a vivid reminder that next, the leaves would fall and the trees would sleep for the winter. They'd come back in the spring, but he wouldn't. He took only cautious comfort in what Cole said about life after death because he still didn't know if it had all been a hallucination. He glanced at his watch once more before throwing his bag into the rental car.

Before starting the drive he remembered, *Time to take another Promaxonex.* Derek eyed the chalky abomination suspiciously. The white oval pill was roughly the size of a Twinkie in Derek's estimation. He nearly gagged it out and required most of his bottle of water to finally wash it down, down, down. As the pill pushed its way through his esophagus, he pitied every snake that ever swallowed a rat. He started questioning the commitment he'd made to Nina when he agreed to take the regimen. If the cancer didn't get him, choking to death on one of these monstrosities just might.

When Derek reached his hometown, he noticed that his old school still stood, proud and timeless, like a red brick sentry over the playground. The iron monkey bars and metal slide had been replaced with bulky, multicolored plastic equipment, but the grounds were still full of screaming kids. He drove past the lemon cream church his parents still faithfully attended every Sunday. He passed the cinder-block grocery store, the post office, the library built during Andrew Carnegie's library-building spree and Mr. Peterson's gas station, all just as Derek had left it. Apart from a few cell phone towers, newer model cars on the road and a Wal-Mart, nothing had changed here.

Derek pulled into the driveway and his heart raced, thinking about what he would say. He exited the car and took deep breaths of the sweet country air, scented with wet leaves and pine, and followed the familiar sidewalk to the front door. He straightened his shirt, wiped his shoes on the porch mat and pushed the doorbell.

His parents met him at the door and took turns with hugs. He had told them a few days ago that his work would be taking him out this way. After catching up in the kitchen for a half hour, sharing stories and recent pictures of the girls, the three all settled on the couch with cups of chamomile tea. Watching his mom hobble to the sofa, smiling through the pain, broke Derek's heart even more than it usually did.

Derek finally found the courage to say, "I've got something I need to ask and something I need to tell you both."

"Alright, honey," Martha encouraged. "Go ahead."

"Mom, I need to ask something of you," Derek said. "Will you forgive me for what I did to you?" His words crumbled and he barely got them out.

"Forgive you for what?" Martha looked at Don who simply shrugged.

"For this," Derek pointed at Martha's hip and leg. "For what I did to you."

"Oh, Derek. Come on now, sugar. Why would you even say such a thing?" Martha waved her hand dismissively and smiled. But she saw in Derek's face the burden he'd carried since the accident. "Derek, I never blamed you for this. Never. It was an accident. It was in God's hands, Derek," Martha grabbed Derek's hands in hers. "Not yours."

"But it was my hands on the wheel of the car," Derek reminded her.

"And it was God's hands on yours," Martha uttered though her voice broke. She understood what he needed and said it, "Of course I forgive you."

Don looked into his teacup and swallowed hard.

His mother's words and touch released him from the prison he'd thrown himself into so long ago. He held her hand to his face, closing his eyes and felt like a child again. His mom's caress after his troubles, fights and tormented days had always been a balm, and was again now. This place truly was just as he'd left it.

As he expected, the news he shared next devastated his parents. He explained his condition, the prognosis and the details, feeling like he'd detonated a grenade in the living room that went off in slow motion. He did his best to tell his parents he'd accepted his fate but knew it would take time for them to feel the same, if they ever did. He was surprised at how calmly he'd explained his illness, but held to the recurring feeling that steadied him—gratitude. Even in these very moments, he was aware of his breath, his parents' every move, the birds singing outside, the sunlight spilling in through the curtains, and he was grateful for it all. Despite the grief of getting and sharing his bad news, he felt truly alive for the first time in his life.

After answering countless questions and offering nearly a box of Kleenex to his parents, Derek finally made his way to his room to unpack. His bedroom had also been frozen in time. When his family had come with him to visit, Nina always got a kick out of the shrine left to Derek's childhood and never ceased to be entertained by the memorabilia and pictures. She told him that she was amazed at how much of a dreamer he had been as a child. Perhaps all those dreams had been beaten out of him over time.

Don and Martha had let Derek paint his own room when he was eleven years old and he did it with relish. Don provided all of the supplies and a dozen cans of paint in a variety of colors. He let Derek know he'd be there if needed, then closed the door behind him. He and Martha slipped away, giggling, and Don admitted he'd always wanted to the same when he was a kid.

Derek painted the entire room sky blue and accented it with puffy white clouds along the upper half of the walls and across the ceiling. After a full weekend of painting, he invited his parents to view the spectacle. Though the walls and ceilings were beautifully done, he stood covered in blue and white paint. The paint had even matted his hair making him look like a character that escaped from the painting. Asked why he had chosen that theme, he remembered shrugging his shoulders and stared lovingly at his walls. "That's where I go when I dream," he remembered saying.

There still hung his poster of a lonesome ribbon of highway reaching into the distant horizon. Above the horizon was an image of a lightning storm in full rage and the caption above it read: *It's out there, waiting for you.* Derek panned around the room at his *Empire Strikes Back* poster, an Oklahoma Sooner football lamp and a rubber troll with electric purple hair teased out to a ridiculous length. Even the bulbous knob on the bed post still lifted off freely when grabbed.

A sudden rush of emotion filled him as he realized Don and Martha hadn't done this for their two sons. As soon as Donnie and Patrick left home, one to join the military and the other to college, Martha converted one room to a reading and sewing area and the other for general storage. But Derek's room had been preserved, perhaps as a reminder to Martha and Don of the restless and often reckless boy that changed their lives so much. Maybe it had been preserved to give that boy a sense of permanence that he'd never known.

Derek lay in bed staring at the ceiling full of clouds. He thought of how easily his mom forgave him and realized he'd been forgiven by her long before he'd asked to be. All those years of guilt and shame carried for what purpose? They had only weighed him down and kept him down. Martha's act inspired him to think of letting go of what others had done to him and what he'd done to himself. Forgiveness didn't seem so impossible to give after seeing how easily his mom granted it.

The three spent the weekend reminiscing about his childhood and taking walks together. Derek often fought the temptation to break out into a run. They also discussed how his death would impact the kids, Nina and the arrangements that would have to be made. Talks of treatment options were cut short after Derek showed his parents his medical records and pictures of the MRI scans and X-rays. They saw quickly what he had come to accept and why he'd accepted it.

Surprisingly, the hardest conversations had less to do with Derek's bleak future and more to do with painful recollections of the past surrounding his childhood. The talks were imbued with regrets that none of them could change. He tried to be uplifting and shared the feelings of thankfulness so strong within him now. He told Don and Martha how he'd made the commitment to enjoy the time and make the most of the moments he had left. He found himself repeating Cole's sentiments in paraphrase about life, death and the most important things.

Martha took comfort in the Bible and read from it throughout the weekend. He was tempted to tell Martha how right the words were, but in the end he knew he didn't need to. His efforts to put on a happy face and reassure his parents seemed to have some success. They ended the visit in a group prayer so moving, Derek felt the familiar beginnings of the electrical buzz.

On the way out of town, Derek noticed the car riding strangely and stopped to find one of the tires nearly flat. *Just terrific* he thought, again glancing at his watch. *Almost Promaxonex time*. He could wait here for an eternity for roadside assistance from the rental car company or change it on his own. He acknowledged he had more money than time, much more, and decided to drive it slowly to a nearby shop. Before he even got out of the car, a balding, rail-thin attendant in a navy blue jumpsuit appeared.

"I don't have to ask what yer here for," he said thrusting his chin in the direction of the tire and spitting tobacco almost the distance. "That'd be twenty-five bucks and about fifteen minutes."

"Sounds good," Derek said, again checking his watch to make sure he'd make the airport on time.

The thin man waved over to his opposite, an obese, unshaven guy wearing two tires on each arm and covered in axle grease. He appeared to be in agony as he hobbled toward them. The only thing the two employees had in common was the jumpsuit. Before the man even spoke, his curly red hair gave him away and Derek saw that when the man grimaced in pain, most of the square, yellowed teeth were missing.

The old enemies recognized each other but their reactions were as different as their appearance. Derek was surprised. Rory McCloud looked like he'd seen a ghost and then seemed embarrassed as his face flushed to match his hair. He couldn't even look at Derek as he spoke.

"Hey there, Derek," he finally said quietly, lowering the tires onto their rack.

"Hey, Rory." A tornado of emotion rose inside. "Been a long time."

Rory nodded and slowly offered his hand forward. Derek looked at it and froze in place, unsure how to react.

"I need your keys so I can drive it into the stall," Rory mumbled.

Derek breathed a sigh of relief.

"Sure," he said. He dropped the keys into Rory's hand.

Derek had so often imagined a grown up Rory in his mind, but never like this. The man in front of him looked conquered and twice his age with twice the wear. The two chatted uncomfortably, trying to act like civil adults but both involuntarily transported back to childhood. In the brief exchange, Derek learned Rory was divorced. He began feeling sorrow for the person he'd hated for as long as he could remember. The boss who had greeted Derek now glared at Rory who was obviously not supposed to be speaking with customers for so long.

"Rory, get back to work!" his boss shouted at him.

Derek thought it ironic that Rory flinched in fear. The warden had become the prisoner.

"Derek. I ..." Rory croaked as he looked up at Derek. "I just ... well."

"Now, damn it!" The boss barked again.

Rory made a fist around the keys, bowed his head and turned toward the car, struggling to shift his girth into the driver's seat.

Derek had entertained fantasies over the years of someday getting a heartfelt apology, complete with tears, from Rory. He always imagined it would be a freeing, glorious event. But this was no cause for celebration or pleasure.

The evil tormentor of Derek's memory, the violent boy responsible for countless cruel acts toward him, had been reduced to an unhappy overweight man with missing teeth.

The chance encounter also spurred Derek to realize he didn't need to hear an apology to forgive. Instead, he made the choice to forgive Rory anyway and a suffocating cloak seemed to fall from his shoulders. Rory, meanwhile, grunted in pain to simply get behind the wheel of a car without getting yelled at again.

CHAPTER 12

DEREK SPENT HIS journey home looking out the window of the airplane and seeing images of the sky and clouds so similar to the ones on the walls of his childhood room. He ached for Nina and the girls, again glancing at this watch to keep track of time. *Precious time.* Though he had no reason to think it, he saw his life as fuller of possibilities than ever before. Despite the diagnosis, despite the lack of time, he felt this to his core. He wanted to make this time count.

He watched the sun turn the clouds into multi-colored scoops of ice cream and smiled with his whole face. He touched the window and closed his eyes, praying a prayer of thankfulness.

He arrived home late and tried his best to be quiet. Nina had left a note on the breakfast bar saying his food was in the refrigerator. He opened the door and light spilled out onto the tile floor. He saw an eclectic combo plate of chicken nuggets, macaroni and cheese, some olives and what looked like a toasted peanut butter and banana sandwich under cellophane. The note on top was a hand-written card reading *compliments of Hannah and Bailey Sorensen* and included flourishes of hearts and smiley faces. Derek chuckled that his girls thought they should include their last name too.

Despite the weird array, he was moved to see the girls worked to make him a plate of their favorite foods.

The next morning was a blur of activity, kisses, laughs and once again, getting the girls ready with Nina. Derek got up early so he could head into work and have another confab with HR about his status before the crowds arrived. He had images in his mind, as he suspected most people did, of what a dying man would do with "X" amount of time to live. The man would quit work, take a decadent vacation around the world and buy a Ferrari. Of course, he would spend time with the people he loved most—but there would definitely be a Ferrari in the driveway.

With his prognosis, so many perspectives on his life had changed, but he was chagrined to see that so many mundane things—paying bills, running errands and waiting in line— remained mundane things. Derek still griped, watched what he spent and went to work. Old, stubborn habits clung to him like barnacles on a ship but made things feel normal.

He volunteered to stay on with Global Medix until they found a replacement for him. He was happy to help in the transition, but mostly, he wanted to avoid being home every day and have Nina feel obligated to attend to him. He knew that time would come too soon. He was trying to not be the dying man of his fantasy, with the Ferrari, but a responsible dying man. He had a family that he loved and was determined to take care of them and make this change as smooth as possible.

He'd noticed since the announcement at work that Skip had been distant and avoiding contact with him. Finally Derek confronted Skip and asked, "You know I've got cancer, right, not leprosy?"

The comment got a weak grin but Skip kept his feet moving down the hall. Derek finally caught Skip in his office, shut the door behind him, and plopped his now lean body in a chair. Skip was cornered.

"What's going on, man?" Derek blurted.

Skip looked out the window, trying to buy time.

"I'm the one dying, but you ..."

"I don't know what it is, Derek. I just don't know how to process all this, what to say," Skip replied. He wiped his chin on his shoulder and sniffed.

"You don't have to know what to say. Just don't cut me out of your life before mine ends."

Skip cringed at the words and Derek suddenly understood why. This was the guy constantly living to fulfill a perfect tomorrow and suddenly the guarantee of that tomorrow had been proved a myth, just as it had when his parents died.

"Dammit, Derek, you're my age," Skip said aloud as if he needed to remind him. "You're not supposed to ..."

"Hey, it happens every minute of every day to someone on the planet. It's only a matter of time for each of us and you don't know when that time will be."

"Yeah, but ..." Skip stammered.

"Listen, Skip, I know you work and work to make your life awesome someday. But someday is now. *Life* is now." Derek grinned after uttering the words. "You've got to stop putting life on hold and start enjoying this gift you have while you have it. Hell, you've probably saved enough to retire already, right?"

Skip snorted.

"You have, you dirty dog," Derek said, pointing his finger at Skip.

Skip shook his head, laughing.

"Seriously, man, life is now. Skip, look at me."

Skip looked up at Derek.

"Life is now. Understand that and it'll be your going away present to me, okay?"

The next day Derek sat on his front porch steps and enjoyed the morning sunshine, tapping the numbers to Sarah's cell. "Good Morning Nurse Pretty on Top," he said as he threw part of his breakfast cereal to a squirrel.

"How've you been?" Sarah asked.

Derek had told her about the diagnosis last week.

"Actually, I've been feeling pretty good," he answered. It was the truth. Maybe he wasn't dying. Maybe he wasn't even sick. Derek knew these musings weren't helpful but he couldn't help having them.

"We're going to miss ..." Sarah stopped short, seeming embarrassed.

Derek was more embarrassed of what slipped out of him: a thunderous, ripping expulsion of bodily gas that vibrated his buttocks on the concrete steps.

"What was that?" Sarah exclaimed.

Derek's face flushed. The squirrel darted for the nearest tree. *Damn Promaxonex.* This spontaneous releasing had been one of the more unsavory side effects in addition to a frequent itching sensation (especially his feet and crotch), crusted-over eyes in the mornings and the occasional strange but pervasive taste in his mouth of grape Kool-Aid. What a wonder drug.

"Um. It was nothing. It was the squirrel I'm feeding."

"Because it sounded more like a ..."

"It was a squirrel," Derek insisted.

He got up and walked into the house as the squirrel chattered angrily from the lowest branch. It was as if the maligned creature heard Derek's false accusation. Derek continued talking with Sarah as he looked out the window at Nina and the girls playing in the backyard.

"Listen, I couldn't get in touch with Arnold, but I thought maybe you could help me out."

"Sure, Derek, what is it?" Sarah asked.

He explained how he'd received the pouch of corn pollen from the elder in Arizona and that he spoke to him in Navajo.

"His grandson told me he needed to give it to me and it was to pray with. Make sense to you?" Derek asked.

Sarah was quiet for a few moments and then answered. "That is a sacred item, Derek. He must have wanted to prepare you for something, getting you ready for the journey ahead."

"But this was before I got the diagnosis," Derek said. "How could he have known?"

"Spirits told him I guess," Sarah answered.

Derek was silent.

"I don't know, Derek. Sometimes the old ones just know things."

After getting off the phone with Sarah, Derek rifled through his drawer to find the bag of corn pollen. He didn't know why, but keeping this sacred item close at hand comforted him.

"Where did I put that thing?" he mumbled to himself, reaching up to the top shelf of the closet for one of his toiletry bags. As he did, Derek bumped a hat box of Nina's and it fell hard onto the floor. The top of the pink and white box flew open and a handful of small brass tubes spilled out onto the carpet from a smaller box hidden within.

"What the ..." Derek began as he picked up the box labeled *Remington .357 Magnum.*

"I'm sorry, Derek," Nina stood in the doorway nervously twisting a lock of her hair. "I wanted to hide them from you because before you'd been so, well. You know."

Derek stood up. He grabbed her hands and pulled her close. "I know," he held her hands tightly. "You don't have to worry about that, Nina."

"It's just that I didn't know what ... if you were thinking about ..." Nina's voice wavered.

"It's okay, honey," Derek said.

His arms swallowed Nina in a fervent hug. He'd never tell her how her actions may have prevented a tragedy. Guilt stung him. What had his behavior put Nina through over the last year? She had been scared enough to hide his bullets from him. What else had she endured?

Derek squeezed Nina as she sobbed in his arms. His thoughts were, over and over again, *My God, I love this woman.*

That evening, as a family, they made pizza. Nina chopped up the olives, onions and mushrooms and Derek did his best chef impression, spinning the dough through the air to the girls' squeals and cheers. Bailey had sauce detail and Hannah was in charge of laying out the pepperoni slices and did so with the meticulous attention of an artist.

Each time Nina glanced at Derek, he pointed at his apron that read *Kiss the Chef* and she obliged each time. The girls tossed olive slices at each other's mouths, hitting everywhere around the kitchen but the intended target.

After dinner Derek plopped onto the couch and the girls scrambled to flank him. Nina still worked in the kitchen.

"Come on, Nina. Come out here and sit with us," Derek said. He dug his fingers into the girls' ribs, causing squirming and laughter. "We'll clean up later."

Nina finally came into the living room holding a giant book. She joined him and the girls on the couch and opened the now completed scrapbook. Page by page they went through their lives together, remembering the moments. Derek and Nina at turns had fits of uncontrollable laughter and then long pauses, trying to stifle emotions. Hannah and Bailey made a game of pointing themselves out in each picture and teasing their parents for looking as young as they did. The scrapbook was beautiful and he could tell Nina must have put countless hours into the project.

The final photo in the album was one they'd taken as a family just a week before at an outdoor table at the Hotel Del Coronado. A perfect moment captured on film. The sun shone and they all seemed to glow in its light.

As Nina closed the back cover, the girls yelled out, "More, more!" Nina and Derek looked at each other, desperately wanting that very thing. The family snuggled closely on the couch together, forgoing the TV, listening to each other's breaths and feeling each other's heartbeats. Even the girls seemed fascinated. Derek embraced them, remembering at how he'd held these two when they were babies, cradling them as the precious treasures they were. Where had the time gone? How right Cole had been—*life is love*. He would miss this the most.

The next morning Derek discussed his work schedule with Nina. They'd decided he'd go to half days so they could spend more time together. According to the doctors' predictions, Derek may or may not make it to Christmas. Derek was torn wanting to spend one more Thanksgiving and Christmas with his family, but he didn't want to die during the holidays either, scarring his girls and Nina forever. Derek wondered about the timing of death. Was there ever a good time?

Derek agreed to make one last trip to Pine Ridge to wrap up a few business items, but also to say goodbye to Sarah, Arnold and Ruby in person. Plus, he had another idea that he couldn't wait to fulfill. The excitement of it reminded him of being a kid on the morning of his birthday. Arnold was in for a big surprise.

Arnold and Derek arrived at the Rapid City Airport and Derek practically bounced off the ceiling of the rental car as they pulled into the parking lot. Arnold squinted as he watched a regional jet coming in to land. Derek invited both Ruby and Arnold to take this flight, but Ruby politely declined. Derek knew this experience was meant to be for just Arnold. The radio aptly played Steve Miller Band's *Jet Airliner* and Arnold thumped his thighs with his thumbs, muttering the lyrics.

"By the way, where *is* this thing carrying us today?" Arnold asked.

"Minneapolis," Derek answered.

Arnold's eyebrows arched up in wonder. "To Minneapolis and back in the same day."

As the two walked to the terminal, Derek reflected on how this had all come to be. When he'd spoken with Ruby and Arnold about his condition, they acted like they'd already known. They sounded saddened and concerned, but not surprised. Derek reflected on Sarah's words, *sometimes the old ones just know things.*

When Derek shared the idea to take them both on a flight, Arnold told him flatly, "I told you Derek, you don't owe us anything."

"I know that, Arnold," Derek said. "I want to do this to satisfy my own gratitude for all you've done."

Arnold looked at Derek and then grinned widely. "Well, in that case, who am I to stand in the way?" Arnold had said, winking at Ruby.

Going through security, Arnold didn't seem to mind a bit that he had to remove his cowboy boots, hat and change from his pockets. Derek guided him through the check-in process and security procedures and Arnold eagerly listened. For someone so wise, so experienced in life, Arnold seemed childlike to Derek in his naiveté in this environment. In fact, he cheerfully did all that was asked. This example humbled Derek, who'd hated this process for years. Arnold, with a fixed grin, seemed only focused on the flight to come, caring little for the sacrifice needed to make it happen.

Derek was retrieving his bag from the conveyer belt when it felt as if he stood in a pile of fire ants, which he'd done once by accident as a kid. *Thanks Promaxonex.* His feet burned and itched, writhing inside his socks. Derek sat down quickly in a chair and desperately scratched at his feet—all under the vacant stare of juvenile TSA agent with sagging slacks and cornrows.

"You're gonna have to remove that," another TSA agent said, looking at Arnold's waist.

Derek chortled even as he furiously itched, seeing the expression of shock on Arnold's face. It seemed Arnold thought the agent asked him to remove his pants.

"The buckle and belt, sir. You have to remove 'em."

Arnold visibly relaxed and removed the enormous metal buckle with accents of green and pink tint, typical of Black Hills gold. It read *Oglala Sioux Open Rodeo Champion 1974.* Arnold walked through the scanner and the alarm sounded.

"Any other metal sir?" the TSA agent asked in monotone.

Arnold considered the question for a moment and said, "Just here." Arnold tapped his head, "And I can't remove that one. Compliments of the Indian Health Service after a bronc named Bonecrusher kicked me in the head."

"Male assist on Lane 1," the TSA droned again, only louder.

The two boarded their first-class seats with Arnold at the window, looking nervous.

"Don't worry, Arnold. It's safer than driving," Derek said.

Arnold turned to Derek and mustered a weak smile.

The part of that flight that would remain in Derek's mind for the rest of his life happened above ten thousand feet. The jet soared through a thick cloud layer and suddenly burst forth from deep gray into a brilliant azure sky filled with bulbous cloud tops that resembled heads of white-haired giants.

Arnold gasped, placing one hand around the small medicine bag hanging around his neck. His eyes glazed over with emotion and wonder. Arnold's other hand reached up slowly to touch the porthole and he whispered, "Beautiful. Amazing. I never thought I'd see ... hau tunkashila (amen Creator)."

When the flight attendant came to their row to ask if they wanted drinks, she stood in silence, watching the Indian elder look out the window and into heaven. Derek sat in awe, seeing the magnificent view through new eyes—Arnold's.

The next morning, Derek lay in bed at the motel, looking at the ceiling, savoring yesterday's flight with Arnold. The last few days had been punctuated with fatigue and a few brief but severe headaches. He wondered how much longer his "good health" would last and how relative that term might be to the doctors who said it.

With a few hours before he was to head home, he decided to take a run. He didn't know how many more he'd be able to do. Still unsure if the voice had been Cole's or his own hallucination, he hadn't tried to reconnect with it in weeks.

There hadn't been much opportunity to run and Derek had been focused on spending as much time as possible with Nina and the girls. He felt much more of this world and wanted to remain here, now more than ever. The voice, whether it was Cole's or his own, represented mortality.

As he laced up his shoes, he wondered what he'd say to his son if he truly was the origin of the voice. Through all the motions to get ready, he did so with more purpose than ever before, aware of each movement, each breath. He held his hand in front of his face, flexing his fingers and twisting his hand. How had he not noticed its complexity and design before?

Derek inhaled the damp air, laced with heavy scents of wood and sage. The morning was crisp and he knew colder days loomed ahead. He took off at a trot, more conscious than ever of the elements surrounding him: the sights, sensations, smells and feelings of his human life. Even the taste of the air itself was nectar to his tongue.

As he accelerated his pace, he reflected on his first, desperate run, and how much his life had changed since then. A trickle of current started in the pit of his stomach. He closed his eyes and smiled, feeling the pleasant flow course throughout his body, the gentle pressure surrounding him. The buzz eventually reached his fingertips and the bottoms of his feet until even his hair was electrified. The sensation became visceral and more complete than ever before. He hoped death would feel this way. He felt a warm presence all around him as he lifted smoothly from the ground. In that moment, he knew this was no hallucination.

"I'm sorry, Cole," Derek said between breaths. "For being so upset with you before. And I wanted to thank you for that dream too. It was so real. It changed everything for me."

"I didn't do that."

"Then what …" Derek stopped mid-sentence. "Well, I've accepted what's going to happen to me." He panned his head around, taking in the scenery. "I just don't want to be alone when it happens. Will you be there, I mean, in the end?"

"Of course, Daddy."

Though curious, Derek didn't want to know any more about the end. Instead, he talked about his conversation with Skip, the flight with Arnold and especially the time with Nina, Hannah and Bailey. He whipped his head sideways to dodge a flying beetle and Cole giggled.

"I've learned so much since you came back. I have a new perspective on … well, on everything." Even though this renewed sense of life was happening too late, it didn't seem in vain to Derek when he said it aloud. Though high above the rolling prairie, he felt more on solid ground than ever in his whole life. A cloud in the distance delivered rain to the dry prairie in long, gray-blue streaks, cascading down like hair.

"I don't think I'll be able to run too many more times with you Cole," Derek admitted.

"I know, Daddy. It's alright. Today is our last day."

The words hit Derek like a wrecking ball.

"Wh-what? Why?" Derek asked.

"I know why I've come back."

Before Derek could question him, Cole spoke again.

"Look down."

Derek did and saw his feet flashing over a small pond surrounded by circling birds far below.

"You don't have to run anymore, Daddy."

A burst of fear shot through Derek's brain, but he trusted Cole and stopped moving his feet. In an intense rush of release, a flood of memories from a lifetime of blessings and pain overwhelmed Derek. His body grew lighter and he rose higher. He flew through the thinning air faster and faster. Wind buffeted his body and made his eyes squint and his hair lie flat. He punched through a small cloud and the moistened air left dew on his face and hands. He outstretched his limbs, truly feeling like a superhero, and laughed hysterically. Everything besides this moment disappeared from his mind. There was no past, no future, just this glorious, wonderful moment.

As they descended, more than gravity pulled him down. Rain fell and he shivered from the wind and wet. Even so, he didn't want this to end. He frantically searched his mind for what to say, knowing his connection with Cole would soon be broken. But when his feet touched the ground, Cole's voice was clear, even over the rain now falling in earnest.

"How was that?" Cole asked brightly.

"Wonderful! It was like being in heav ..." Derek's heart jumped wildly, realizing what had been there all along. "I think I know why you've come back too," he said cautiously. "You came back for me," he shouted over the developing storm.

Cole's silence unnerved Derek.

"It's today isn't it?" he said as he shielded his eyes from the rain. "My time is over and you've come to take me."

"No, Daddy. That's not why I've come back."

Derek hunched his shoulders in the onslaught of biting rain.

"It was to give back to you what I took with me when I left," Cole continued.

"I don't understand, Cole," Derek yelled.

"Faith."

A deafening blast of thunder exploded as lightning hit nearby but Derek didn't move.

"You asked me before why I was taken from you and Mom. I told you I chose to leave."

"Yes. I remember."

"I chose to leave because when I was born you leaned over me and I saw something inside of you. I love you, Daddy, and if I stayed I couldn't help you."

Derek realized his cancer had been present when Cole was born.

"I chose to leave so I could come back for this ..."

All of a sudden, Derek's head filled with a teeth-jarring hum. It felt like parts of his brain were expanding out beyond the boundary of his skull and then those parts were being plucked, like feathers, from his head. The sky around him erupted and filled with white and purple lighting but Derek could only hear the loud hum and whispering. His head seemed ready to split open at the seams as a wave of nausea hit him hard, dropping him to his knees. Suddenly, everything went quiet, save the gentle patter of a light rain on the wet ground around him. The air smelled of ozone from the lighting strikes. The nausea abated and he felt used up, like he'd just climbed a mountain. Warmth enveloped him.

With trembling lips, Derek asked, "Cole, did you just do what I think ..." and then realized he didn't have to. He already knew the answer. He could feel it. The cancer was gone.

"Will I see you, or be with you again?" Derek couldn't fight the desperation in his voice.

"Yes. I've always been with you ... not just in the NICU, and not just here and now ... I was with you in the woods when you were lost as a boy."

Memories locked away for so long came all at once. The flashes flickered like an abruptly spliced reel of movie film—the brutal beating, running away, being hungry and shivering in the cold for days, but feeling that someone was with him. No. He *knew* someone was with him, watching over him, and now he knew the truth.

Derek looked at his open hands in front of him in pure amazement. His hands, arms and entire body were releasing steam as the moisture evaporated off him just as it had when he was a boy lost in the woods. He blinked the rain out of his eyes to better see a clear, ethereal form appearing in front of him, only visible because of the raindrops hitting its surface. Derek wiped his face and shook his head, not believing what he was seeing—the familiar face of a baby. It was Cole. He watched, kidnapped by the moment, as the face transformed into that of a toddler, then a boy. Derek couldn't breathe, realizing he was getting to see what had been taken away. The translucent figure changed slowly to that of a teen and finally morphed into a face that looked much like his own, as if he was staring at a glass version of himself. He leaned forward to be closer and the face started changing again, regressing until it was again Cole as a baby. He reached his hands toward the image as it disappeared.

Derek fell onto his hands and knees, crying with the rain and with the finality of healing he'd wished for so long. His son had come back to save Derek's life in every sense of what meaning those words possessed.

EPILOGUE

THE FOLLOW-UP DOCTOR appointments in the
weeks that followed confirmed what Derek already knew—the
dark tentacles had lost their grip and his cancer was gone. The
doctors were baffled, surprised at how effective Promaxonex was.
Nina was still in shock, his daughters never knew he had been sick,
and Arnold was the only one who seemed to understand any of it.
Even Derek still bobbed in the swells of the aftermath. As he
packed, he looked at the statuette of the angel with the wire wings
on his dresser and smiled. The angel held a baby boy in her arms—
his baby boy.

Derek knew the things he'd learned and relearned were
burned into his mind and spirit for the rest of his life. Everything
was different now. He still had Nina, Hannah and Bailey, his parents and his friends, but the way he saw these gifts was completely
changed. The light of the lessons he'd learned illuminated all he
had, who he was, and it was the difference between a slice of stale
bread and one of Arnold's gourmet meals. He now had a future
and he made a commitment to himself and his Creator that he
would do all in his power to make it good—not just for himself,
but also for his family and all those around him. Reborn into his

life, he was determined not to squander the gift he'd been given. Not this time.

And thank God, no more Promaxonex.

A few weeks later, Derek, yet again, reviewed his list and made sure all the gifts were in order. "Flashlights, blankets, pots and pans," he mumbled as he walked down the line of boxes in the hallway. "Nina," he yelled in no particular direction. "Honey, where are the toys?"

He turned around and Nina bumped into him. She shook her head, smiling, and Derek knew why.

"I know, I know. I've just never done this before and I'm kind of ..."

"Derek, it's going to be fine," Nina said, placing her hands on his shoulders. "Don't worry. Plus, you probably have the list memorized by now."

Derek nodded thoughtfully, missing the joke.

"And the girls are downstairs inspecting the toys," Nina continued. "You know, to make sure we chose well."

The sound of kazoos, tambourines and riotous laughter made it upstairs.

"I think that's a 'yes' vote." Nina said.

The family was excited to make the journey to South Dakota on the invitation of Arnold and Ruby. They'd invited them because they had something very special for Derek—a naming ceremony and an adoption ceremony, called the making of relatives or *hunkapi.*

Arnold understood Derek never found the tribe to which he belonged. He also understood how that hole in Derek's spirit might never be filled so he'd talked to his people and Derek and arranged this ceremony. An Indian without a tribe was like a tree without roots, and from their conversations, Arnold believed some of Derek's struggles stemmed from this lack of identity. Ruby now called him *takosha* or grandson, and this ceremony was the best gift they could give him.

Derek was elated but knew this role had responsibilities too. He would be of a people now. His adoption meant he would also be adopting the *tiospaye* as well, all the people. Though Derek didn't know what to expect, he was eager nonetheless.

The morning breeze made the leaves on the trees dance. The sky was a cornflower blue and accented with cotton ball clouds, identical to the room Derek had painted so long ago. He stood shirtless, wearing shorts and flip flops, waiting for Arnold and the medicine man, Marcus Walking Bear, to enter the sweatlodge.

"Come on in now, Derek," Arnold motioned from inside the lodge. Outside, fire keepers moved rocks around in the fire with pitchforks, making a high pitched twang. Stepping out of his flip flops, Derek crawled into the inipi. The lodge, much warmer only because it was out of the wind, would be hot soon.

Marcus Walking Bear had a spotted chest from the raised lumps of Sun Dance scars, like Arnold's. Derek guessed Marcus to be at least eighty years old with long, thinning white hair and a face of countless wrinkles. The man's manner put Derek at ease immediately. His stomach quivered as he wondered what the day would bring, what his new name would be. He received a reassuring grin from Arnold as he and Marcus guided the rocks into the lodge. Warmth filled the cavern and Derek prayed as the flap closed over the doorway.

Many hours later, after the naming ceremony was completed, everyone was assembled next to a creek. Derek felt completely alone as he looked skyward, though he was surrounded by nearly a hundred people, including his family, in a stand of swaying cottonwoods. Shafts of sunlight shot through the openings in the thick foliage onto a sun-dappled ground. The smoke from burning sage and sweetgrass laced through the trees like dancing ghosts. Derek was flanked by Marcus, Arnold and Ruby on one side and Nina and the girls on the other. In front of them were the inviting faces of the Lakota *oyate* (people)—soon to be Derek's new family members.

Marcus Walking Bear cleared his throat and began praying in Lakota. Everyone lowered their heads in unison.

"This man will be our brother and he will be yours," Marcus said. The people nodded in agreement. "From now on, you will be responsible for him and he for you. This is what makes us Lakota, what makes us tiospaye or family. I present your hunka, your relative. His given name is 'Runs with the Spirits'."

The old ones truly did know things Derek thought as Arnold and Ruby draped a Pendleton blanket around his shoulders, symbolizing the embrace of a people, his new relatives. The whispering breeze was shattered with the crash of the opening drumbeat of an honoring song and the sound of ladies trilling in celebration.

That night Derek and Nina held hands and walked on the edges of the main encampment, gazing at the stars. Bailey and Hannah were in good hands, being looked after by their extended family and playing with a dozen of their new cousins.

"Another bowl of buffalo stew for your thoughts," Nina said.

"Oh, please no," Derek joked and held his hand over his belly, still filled from the feast. He reached down and plucked a long blade of prairie grass and watched it dance as he rolled it between his fingertips.

"I know what I want to do but not how to do it. I don't want to go back to Global Medix."

This was no big surprise to Nina and she nodded.

"I want to do something involving running. And kids. Maybe foster kids." Derek's eyes lit up and a nervous smile spread across his face. "To help them the way it's helped me, you know? Yeah, maybe foster kids or something. I'm not sure, I just …"

"It's okay, Derek. You don't have to know," Nina said as she squeezed his hand. "We'll figure it out. I think it sounds wonderful."

"And I think Skip is going to help me out too," Derek said.

"Really?"

"Well, he says he's ready for a change too and the idea really connected with him. Plus, he's got some great funding ideas, a mini-marathon concept for youth and plus, you know, he ran track in high school and with his business planning background …"

Nina poked Derek in the ribs.

"Listen to you, Mr. I'm-not-sure," she bumped his shoulder with hers. "You've already got this all figured out!"

Derek threw his head back and laughed, looking up at a sky filled with twinkling beacons. Just then a fiery white tail appeared, running across the entire sky. The falling star reminded him of what someone very wise shared with him not so long ago. All that we do, the journey we walk, can lead to a beautiful and lasting memory to those who witness it. … *That pretty flash you remember forever.* His head was filled with new ideas and directions on how he would create this in his life, but one undeniable urge overcame Derek. It was time to share the truth with Nina. About everything.

"Nina?" Derek took both her hands in his and looked deeply into her star-sprinkled eyes. "I have something else I really need to share with you …"

… Derek continues to run. He might be running right now. But he no longer runs to get away from things. He runs for his peace, his health and simply because he enjoys it. Derek runs in the sunshine, the rain, the wind and in the night. He runs on days he doesn't especially feel like it because he always feels better afterward. He feels *he's* better afterward. He runs for many reasons, but he always runs with the idea buried deep in his mind that someday, perhaps in a perfect moment, just maybe ...

But until then, he makes this a good life each day because it is, indeed, a beautiful gift.

For Kieran Cruz Vanas
September 21, 2003–September 27, 2003
In his short time, he reminded us that life is love, life is now and
life is a beautiful gift.

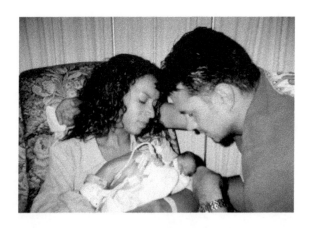

About the Author

D.J. Vanas was born to teenage parents in poverty, slept in a dresser drawer for the first three months of his life. When finally moved to a crib, he mumbled for hours at a time to the baby on the Pamper's box that his mom placed near to keep him company, showing a passion to share his message right from the beginning ...

Now, he is an internationally-acclaimed motivational speaker and a leadership and personal development expert that shows organizations how to practically apply the power of the warrior spirit to perform at their best, stay resilient and thrive in tough, changing environments. For two decades, he has delivered his dynamic pro-grams in 49 states and overseas to over 5,000 audiences including Walt Disney, NASA, Wells Fargo, Boston Children's Hospital, United States Secret Service, Subaru, Costco and hundreds of tribal governments, communities and schools. He's also been invited to the White House to speak—twice.

D.J. is also the author of the celebrated book *The Tiny Warrior: A Path to Personal Discovery & Achievement* which is now printed is six countries.

D.J. is a tribally-enrolled member of the Odawa Nation and a former military officer. He is a veteran Sun Dancer and his given name in traditional ceremony is Mato Wambli (Eagle Bear).

He holds a B.S. from the U.S. Air Force Academy and an M.S. from the University of Southern California, has been a member of the National Speaker's Association since 1997 and currently serves as a board member on the National Board of Certified Counselors. He is also the founder and president of Native Discovery Inc.

He lives with his wife Arienne and daughters Gabrielle and Isabella in Colorado.

Visit www.djvanas.com to learn more about D.J. Vanas and his programs or call Native Discovery Inc. at 719-282-7747.

CPSIA information can be obtained
at www.ICGtesting.com
Printed in the USA
JSHW031526150820
7291JS00002BA/8